“What kind of list

She tapped the pen against her pursed lips.
I’ll call it Lilly’s Christmas List.”

Lilly stopped playing and looked at Jenny. “My Christmas?”

“That’s right.” She turned in her seat to face Eric. “I’m not only going to help you do Christmas right, I’ll have you loving it.”

He groaned. This sounded like way too much time spent together. And a risk to his sanity and personal space. And he liked a lot of personal space. “Maybe what we already have is enough.”

“Daddy, I want a Christmas magic.” Lilly spread her arms wide. “A lot and a lot.”

Jenny laughed, then bit her lip when she caught his stare. *Sorry*, she mouthed. “But I’ll make it fun. I promise.”

He didn’t want her promise. Promises were fragile things that were too easily broken. But what was he supposed to do with the two of them staring at him with hopeful gazes? “Looks like I’ll be buying more decorations,” he said on a sigh. “If my Lilly Bug wants a big Christmas, I’ll make it happen.”

His daughter’s smile flooded him with love, but when he glanced at the glowing grin of the woman across the table, he momentarily forgot how to breathe. He could not get wrapped up in this acting-like-a-family stuff.

Dear Reader,

Welcome back to Oak Hollow! *A Child's Christmas Wish* is the third book in my Home to Oak Hollow series. While writing, I have fallen in love with this small Texas Hill Country town and its welcoming residents. Each book in this series celebrates parents of children with unique needs. From personal experience, I understand the fortitude and patience sometimes needed while parenting but also the great joy and love.

When single father Eric McKnight moves into a historic home in Oak Hollow, he hires a nanny for his three-year-old daughter, who has cerebral palsy. He's extremely cautious with his and his daughter's hearts, and no one has ever accused him of being Mr. Christmas. Jenny Winslet has been saving money for years, and this temporary position is her long-awaited ticket to design school. But until she leaves, she'll focus on teaching this grinchy guy how to do Christmas right for his precious daughter. Can she reach his guarded heart while discovering true love and the power of Christmas wishes?

If you enjoy *A Child's Christmas Wish*, be sure to check out the first two books in this series, *A Sheriff's Star* and *In the Key of Family*. I love connecting with readers, and you can find all of my social media at makennalee.com. As always, thank you for reading!

Best wishes,

Makenna Lee

A Child's Christmas Wish

MAKENNA LEE

Recycling programs for this product may not exist in your area.

ISBN-13: 978-1-335-40813-6

A Child's Christmas Wish

This edition published by arrangement with Harlequin Books S.A.

For questions and comments about the quality of this book, please contact us at CustomerService@Harlequin.com.

Harlequin Enterprises ULC
22 Adelaide St. West, 40th Floor
Toronto, Ontario M5H 4E3, Canada
www.Harlequin.com

Printed in U.S.A.

Makenna Lee is an award-winning romance author living in the Texas Hill Country with her real-life hero and their two children. Her writing journey began when she mentioned all her story ideas and her husband asked why she wasn't writing them down. The next day she bought a laptop, started her first book and knew she'd found her passion. Makenna is often drinking coffee while writing, reading or plotting a new story. Her wish is to write books that touch your heart, making you feel, think and dream.

Books by Makenna Lee

Harlequin Special Edition

Home to Oak Hollow

The Sheriff's Star
In the Key of Family

Visit the Author Profile page
at Harlequin.com for more titles.

To my parents, Margaret and Forrest, and all the moms and dads who are blessed with a child who needs a little extra attention and understanding.

Chapter One

This guy really needs me. But what am I getting myself into?

Tendrils of smoke, and the acrid scent of burned food drifted from the open kitchen door of Barton Estate. Jenny Winslet considered running back to the warmth of her car, but this single father obviously needed a nanny. When police chief Anson Curry had approached her about this job, she'd almost declined, but with the amount of money Eric McKnight was offering for only a couple of months, she'd finally have enough saved to begin fashion design school at the spring semester.

She continued across the redbrick patio as a rich baritone voice mingled with the remains of smoke. The a cappella recording reminded her of her grandmother's favorite singer, Frank Sinatra, and cemented her original prediction that the man who'd purchased Barton Estate would be a clean-cut gentleman in khakis and a button-up. Someone who attended the opera and drank fine bottles of wine.

But when she stood in the open doorway, it was not the radio or a recording. *Wowzer.* The voice was coming from the mountain of a man standing at the stove with a toddler on his hip. His rich, full voice was so big it drowned out the whirr of the vent fan and filled the space between them. He turned enough that she caught a view of his face.

Holy heart rush.

He was a Highland warrior with the voice of an angel, and Jenny was surprised he didn't have a claymore strapped to his back. His brown hair reached his shoulders, the strands streaked with sun-bleached highlights. The kind one gets from working outdoors, not a bottle. He was *Outlander*'s Jamie, Aquaman and Thor all rolled into one delicious treat for the eyes.

But he was s-o-o-o off limits.

Getting involved with the man who wrote her paycheck could risk the last step in securing her ten-year dream.

The adorable curly-headed toddler tipped her head and returned Jenny's smile over the giant's shoulder.

Maybe he wasn't her prospective boss and wouldn't be forbidden. Maybe he was…

A delicious figment of my imagination?

The tempting man stopped singing. "Lilly Bug, it looks like we're having a can of soup tonight."

Of course he has a dreamy speaking voice, too.

Jenny's inner diva stood up and fluttered her lashes. Even her Pollyanna-good-girl side fanned her face. Why was she so attracted to guys who looked like bad boys, and usually had an equally bad effect on her heart?

The little girl's tiny hand patted his flannel-covered shoulder. "Daddy, look see. Fairy girl."

His broad chest lifted on inhale, eyes making a quick sweep of Jenny's body before widening.

Suddenly breathless and overheated, she locked in on his gaze and couldn't look away. Her grandmother would say they were gawking like a pair of lusty teens. And she'd be right. Resistance was going to be…tough.

"You a fairy girl," the toddler squealed, making her father wince and breaking the connection with Jenny.

She stepped over the threshold. "Hello there. You must be Lilly."

After a delighted gasp, the cutie giggled behind her hand.

A happy child was always a good sign. This situation couldn't be as dire as she'd first feared.

"Are you Jenny?" he asked, his voice a deep rumble, but with a noticeable coolness.

"Yes, sorry. I should've knocked and introduced myself." She rushed forward with her hand extended but dropped it when his free hand fisted at his side. Brows that had been arched in surprise now drew together, and pale blue eyes with dark outer rings narrowed into a penetrating stare. She shivered, and it wasn't from the cold November air coming in the open doorway. It was a shot of lust so strong she worried she'd blush to her toes.

Nope. Get control. Resist. All. Temptations.

Shifting until the marble-topped kitchen island stood between them, she tugged at the neck of her red cable-knit sweater and was tempted to press her fingertips to her lips. Jenny's heart—so recently healed—was still in self-protect mode. "If this is a bad time, I can come back tomorrow." If she didn't pull herself together in a big hurry, she was bound to say something embarrassing.

"Now is as good of a time as any. I'm Eric McKnight, but I guess you've figured that out." Shifting his daughter on his hip, he motioned to the smoking remains on the stovetop. "I would offer you dinner, but..."

"I already ate but thank— Oh!" Jerking up her hand and spinning, she discovered the upturned face and wagging tongue of a golden retriever.

Lilly giggled, and her father's brows sprang up again. "Are you afraid of dogs?"

"No. I love animals."

"That's Brad," Eric said. "He's Lilly's therapy dog."

"He's quiet on his feet and just startled me." She knelt and stroked his soft fur. "Hello. It's nice to meet you." She laughed when the animal held up a paw for a shake.

"I hope you don't mind discussing the nanny position while I feed Lilly?"

"Not at all. In fact, let me help." Jenny crossed to the stovetop but hesitated when he stiffened and stepped away. The single father who'd stared at her with what felt like sizzling attraction was now scowling, and the vibe was not one of mutual attraction. A stab of disappointment tightened her belly. Just because she couldn't date him didn't mean she wanted him to find her unattractive. "Why don't I toss out the...uhm." The charcoal blobs on the cookie tray were not easily identifiable.

"Chicken strips and tater tots," he said and glanced away.

Lilly waved a hand in front of her nose. "Yucky stinky."

"Let's get this smelly stuff out of here." Grabbing two potholders, Jenny took the tray, headed out the still-open door to the edge of the back parking area near the carriage house and tossed the burned food into a thicket of trees. The neglected structure of what had been a fantastical playhouse was still nestled in the overgrown woods. Once upon a time it had been a little girl's dream. A one-room miniature version of a fine house, complete with lacy curtains and a chandelier. But time, weather and forgotten summers had stolen the magic. The place that had held such fascination for an imaginative little girl was now overgrown and weathering away with each season, but that couldn't hide her faded childhood memories.

When she turned back for the house, Eric's frame

filled the window above the sink. And his expression… Searching. Curious. Brooding. She was good at reading people, but this guy…

The man was a mystery. And Jenny loved a good mystery. This one would be especially fun to solve *if* she was doing that. Which she wasn't. She hurried her steps and willed the brisk wind to blow away her off-limits thoughts.

Lilly was seated in a booster seat eating Goldfish crackers while her delectable and somewhat intimidating father dumped a can of beef stew into a pot.

"What was it?" he asked.

"What?" She put the dirty tray into the sink, unsure if she'd missed part of his question while preoccupied with thoughts that could lead her into trouble of the heartache kind.

"In the woods. What held your attention for so long?"

To keep from staring at his piercing eyes, she focused on washing her hands. "An old playhouse I remember from childhood. Sadly, it's starting to deteriorate from lack of care."

"I thought it was a storage shed because it's full height. You've been here before?"

"Yes." She took a seat at the table beside the precious toddler who cocked her head and handed Jenny a cracker. "Thank you, Lilly. My grandmother, Mimi, used to cook for Mrs. Barton, and I often came with her."

"So, you know this kitchen?"

"Quite well. I've spent a lot of time in this house." This kitchen had played a big part in her growing up. She had great memories of running around and playing in the butler's pantry when she was about Lilly's age. Mimi's singing as she cooked. The aroma of baking bread and fresh butter melting on her tongue. Homework at the kitchen table. And Mrs. Barton sneaking her treats while Mimi was pretending not to see it.

"You like fairies?" Lilly whispered.

"I love fairies." She couldn't resist stroking the toddler's soft, blond curls. "How old are you?"

"I'm a big girl," she said and shared another cracker.

"You sure are."

"She's almost four," Eric said and knelt to give the dog a treat and belly rub.

As she did when she got nervous, Jenny started to chatter. "Anson said you're going to remodel this place. Unfortunately, Jim, the town's best and only full-time remodeler recently retired. He's the one who painted the outside of this house right before you bought it. His old crew still does some of the work, but not full renos. You'll have to venture to a nearby town to hire a good company."

"That won't be necessary. I'm a construction contractor. Had my own company in Chicago." He handed a sippy cup of juice to his daughter. "I'd like to talk to some of Jim's craftsmen and see if any of them are interested in working for me."

"I went to high school with a few of them and can introduce you." So, that's where he got all the bulging muscles and highlights. Construction. She had been wrong on so many accounts for what she'd expected. "Do you plan to keep the historical features or modernize this house?"

"I want to focus on historically accurate restoration."

Excitement took away some of her jumpiness and gave her hope that they'd have something in common to talk about. "That's wonderful news. This house has such elegant lines and shapes. The movement from one space to the next is so flowing and inviting."

He paused stirring the soup to glance in her direction. "That's an interesting way to put it."

Unable to hold his gaze without blushing, she focused on the built-in baker's cabinet where she'd helped Mimi knead dough and cut out sugar cookies. So many nice memories filled this house. "I tend to think in shapes and lines. Always have."

"More, please," Lilly said and kicked one leg.

"Just a few, Lilly Bug," Eric said and poured two glasses of tea. "Stew is almost ready."

Jenny grabbed the bag from the table and sprinkled some onto the plate. "There you go, sweetie. What made you decide to move to Oak Hollow and buy this big old house?"

"Anson Curry."

"He said you were a friend but didn't say from where."

"Marines."

If she'd known this, she might've been prepared for the tough and sexy man of few words she'd met as opposed to the one she'd expected.

"When this place went on the market, he called. He's been trying to get me to move here ever since..." Eric cleared his throat. "For a while now."

What had he stopped himself from saying? Could it be the mother no one had mentioned? Now didn't seem the time for an inquiry. She needed to get her nerves under control and make sure he knew she was capable of taking care of his daughter. "Tell me what you expect in a nanny."

"I was thinking..." He scratched his cheek, a hint of stubble whispering under his fingers. "I had thought about a live-in nanny, but you'd probably be more comfortable at your own place?"

It was stated as a question, as if he were as unsure about things as she was. Living in this house? With him? Sleeping under the same roof? With the funny little sparks shooting through her, it was probably best if she wasn't here at night. "I can just come during the day if that's best. And Anson told you that I can only work for a short time?"

"Yes. Something about school?" Eric put a glass of tea in front of her.

"Fashion design school in New York City."

"Eager to get away from here?" He attached a red

plastic bowl with a suction cup bottom to the table in front of Lilly.

"I've been trying to get out of my hometown for years." As beautiful as it was here, she looked forward to being beyond the borders of the Texas Hill Country. Among culture and high fashion. "I can't wait to explore more of the world."

His brows slashed into a deep V, and his upper lip cocked right before a barely audible growl slipped out.

Whoa. Jenny shivered. What had she said to garner this animalistic reaction? It both startled and turned her on in equal measure. This man made her think of a lion, powerful, gorgeous and dangerous. She had the sudden urge to touch and calm him. Tame him. See if she could make him purr.

Stop it, girl!

He lifted his daughter's left arm onto her tray. "Use this hand to get your cracker." He pushed a goldfish closer, and she grabbed it with two fingers. "Now put it in your mouth."

The toddler brought it first to her chest and then to her mouth.

Jenny realized Lilly tended to favor her right arm. "Anson told me she'll be starting physical therapy soon?"

"First session is in a few weeks. Her left side is weaker due to cerebral palsy, especially her leg. I first noticed when she was learning to roll over and push herself up."

She recalled Tess Curry's protective nature with her daughter, Hannah, and how quickly Anson had taken to raising a child with Down syndrome. Jenny was well aware of what parents of any special needs child often went through. Issues most parents never considered. Worries that weighed heavy on a heart and mind. It was clear that Eric needed her help. She couldn't walk away just because he made her feel everything at once. "I can learn and help with the exercises they suggest."

He released a breath. "That would be great. Can you cook?"

Captured by his hopeful expression, it took her a moment to put together the right words. "Yes, I can. Lucky for you and this kitchen." *Oh flip! Why'd I say that last part?*

A slow half smile lifted one corner of his mouth. "No doubt."

The breath eased from her chest on a small shiver. There was a sense of humor under his grumbly facade.

"So, will you be Lilly's nanny?"

"Yes. Absolutely." Lilly was adorable with a capital *A* and would be a pleasure to take care of, but Eric McKnight...

He was going to be a multilevel challenge.

Once they had the logistics of her new nanny position worked out, Jenny drove straight to Sip & Read, the new wine bar and bookstore on the town square.

The Halloween decorations had been removed, leaving behind pumpkins and fall leaf garlands that fluttered in the autumn wind. What had once been a hardware store now boasted a historically elegant vibe with red brick walls, dark woodwork and unique book displays. Each genre was combined with appropriately themed merchandise and beverage suggestions.

Girls' night with Tess and Alexandra was her favorite night of the week. She joined her friends at their usual table in the romance section. "Tess Curry, why didn't you warn me about your husband's military buddy?"

The other woman's big green eyes widened. "I haven't met him yet. What's wrong with him?"

"Oh, this sounds like it'll be good," Alexandra said and adjusted the thin paintbrush holding her long auburn hair in a messy bun.

Tess slid a glass of red wine across the table to Jenny. "Tell us. Judging by the sparkle in your eyes, it couldn't be that bad."

"He's one of those swallow-your-tongue-smokin'-hot-manly-man types. Picture Jason Momoa as a Highland warrior. And he sings like a professional."

"He sang to you?" her girlfriends said in unison and smiled big cheesy grins.

"Not to me." Funny little tingles danced in her belly as her active imagination spun a tale of his piercing blue eyes locked on hers while he crooned a love song.

"Yoo-hoo, Earth to Jenny," one of the women said.

With a shake of her head, she returned from fantasyland. "He was singing to his daughter when I got there." That garnered a round of *Awws*.

"My husband has been holding out on me." Tess tipped her glass of wine in a cheers motion. "Tell us everything, sparing no details."

Jenny sighed and propped her chin on her fist. "I'm going to be tripping over my feet and my tongue every time he comes into the room. But his little girl is adorable and called me fairy girl. I couldn't say no to taking care of her. Lilly is only three, but since they're new in town, maybe we can set up a play date with Hannah and Cody."

"Absolutely," Tess said. "You know how much Hannah loves to play the little momma to younger children."

"So..." Alexandra leaned closer and lowered her voice. "Did this hot, single daddy flirt with you?"

Jenny's bark of laughter held no real amusement. "He definitely did not flirt with me. Not in the least little bit. Although I was instantly attracted to him, he seemed repelled by me."

"What? No way," Tess said.

"It's true. He didn't want to shake my hand, backed away when I got close and his facial expressions screamed more of a warning than come here and kiss me."

Alexandra chuckled and rubbed her paint-stained hands together. "I think I know what's going on.

That's exactly how Luke acted when we first met. I believe we have a case of he's so attracted to you that you scare the boots off him."

"I don't think so." Jenny said.

"I think we need to set up more than a play date." Tess's wide full-watt smile showed off her dimples. "I'll tell Anson to invite this mysterious man over for Thanksgiving. We can check out the way he looks at you."

"Good idea," Alexandra said. "Since we'll all be there, it's the perfect opportunity."

Jenny loved that these amazing women had become such good friends, but they were way too eager to see her settled down, just like them. "This is not a request to fix me up," Jenny scolded and took a large sip of wine. "It's a plea to help me resist my new boss until I leave for New York."

"Oh, that reminds me," Alexandra said. "My aunt and uncle said the construction of their garage apartment will be done before the start of the design school's next session. And as long as you're willing to house and pet sit during all of their upcoming travels, you stay there rent free."

Something fluttered in Jenny's chest. "That's amazing news. If they're truly serious, I'll absolutely take that deal."

"They're very serious. They plan to travel a lot over the next few years and want someone there. Just remember that you'll have to take the subway to go to school."

"It sounds exciting and so different from what I'm used to. Alexandra, I can't thank you enough for setting this up." This extremely generous offer would not only stretch Jenny's savings so much further, but realistically make it possible for her to actually attend design school in New York.

"I'm really going to miss you, but we're all so proud and excited for you. You're finally chasing your dream." Tess stroked the sapphire velvet cape draped over her chair. "Even though I don't know what design school can teach you that you don't already know. For example, this beautiful garment. Everyone wants to know where I bought it."

"Right?" Alexandra said. "Everything you make is killer. You don't just make clothes, you create them."

The compliment made Jenny smile. "I'm sure there's plenty for me to learn. Not to mention the credibility the degree will provide." Jenny had made up her mind years ago. She'd go to design school and hopefully work for a big fashion house. That was the plan. "So, what are your husbands and children up to tonight?"

"Wait. Back up a minute." Alexandra glanced around and then leaned closer. "Why do you need to resist this hot new guy?"

Jenny twitched a finger in the air. "Don't be putting ideas in my head. He's my boss, and I can't risk not getting this paycheck. Plus, I'm leaving soon. And he doesn't like me." She'd keep telling herself that. It would make it easier to resist anything happening between them.

Her girlfriends shared a look as if marriage had given them special knowledge and powers in the relationship department.

"Don't rule anything out," Tess said. "Take it from ladies who have been in your position."

"You didn't work for your husbands."

Alexandra laughed. "True, but we haven't seen this kind of excitement from you since before that bozo who shall not be named broke your heart."

Jenny couldn't argue that truth. That bozo had played with her emotions, and she was glad he'd moved across the country.

As for the man still in Oak Hollow? Eric would be a daily treat for her eyes, and at the same time, a workout in controlling temptation.

Chapter Two

His daughter was sound asleep, but Eric McKnight continued to stare at the front cover of Lilly's favorite storybook, the one he'd read every single night for the past three weeks. Jenny did look a little like the fairy in the story. An adult version with long shiny black hair flowing around soft skin, pink cheeks, red lips and…

Stop it, fool. You know better.

Jenny's statement about exploring the world had struck a wounded place inside him. A wound as old as his first memories. Her words had been the splash of reality needed to remind him what could happen when he got too close to someone. Anyone. Growing up in the foster care system had taught him to hold his emotions close, and he usually had no trouble hiding his feelings. What was it about Jenny Winslet that made his protective shield slip?

The potent reaction she stirred needed to be put on the "hard no" list, fast. Jenny was a temporary employee who he'd treat as such and make sure no lines were crossed, and no connections were made that could end in him or his daughter feeling abandoned for something better, again.

Why couldn't she be married or eighty years old? Better yet, a guy. And why hadn't Anson warned him that he was going to have one hell of a time being around her?

He kissed Lilly's golden curls, scented with baby shampoo and an underlying note of something sweet. "Sleep well, baby girl. Daddy loves you." This amazing little person was the only one in the world who truly loved him, maybe ever. He patted the foot of the bed, and Brad jumped onto his spot. "Watch over our girl."

The animal leaned into a good head scratching and then settled down as silent sentry.

He stepped around boxes of toys that still needed unpacking. Once he was out of earshot, he dialed Anson's number, and his buddy picked up after two rings.

"Hey, McKnight. How are you settling in?"

"You could've warned me. I was expecting Jenny to be the grandmotherly type, and you sent me a woman who…" Not wanting to reveal the visions in his head, he pulled a beer from the refrigerator and flicked the top into the trash. His buddy's familiar chuckle told him he already knew what he was thinking and was enjoying his discomfort. "I hope this isn't your idea of a setup."

"Honestly, I only referred Jenny because she's fantastic with kids," Anson said. "But now that you've brought it up, it wouldn't hurt you to get back in the game."

Eric stepped outside into the cold night air. The silence of the country would take some getting used to after years of living in downtown Chicago. "Just because you've gone all family man on me doesn't mean I have to follow you back into it. I can handle my own love life."

"I hear you. Just remember, I've been in some version of your relationship hell, and I know how hard it is after getting the rug pulled out. Now that you and Lilly are in Oak Hollow, I hope you can put some of those things behind you."

"Yeah. Me, too." Which was exactly why he could not hook up with the first woman in town to trigger his sex drive. And he'd try not to think about how the new nanny had reached in and done a lot more than just catch his eye. She made uncomfortable feelings tighten his chest. The kind of feelings that had caused him more hurt than he cared to remember.

"Jenny is a sweet girl," Anson said. "I've known her since she was born."

"That must be why you call her a girl." It was not the term that came to mind when Eric thought of his tempting new employee. "How old is she?"

"Twenty-seven, and I sent her for Lilly, not for your pleasure," Anson said as if reading Eric's mind.

"Bro, you know me better than that. I'll respect her." There was more than one guy he'd set straight for disrespecting women. He took a long pull on his beer.

"I know you will." Anson's sigh drifted over the phone line. "I didn't mean to imply anything."

He hadn't taken offense and was honestly surprised his buddy hadn't started with that warning. Chief Curry had always been a fierce protector, even the first time they'd met and Eric had needed a friend. "She's lucky to have you looking out for her."

"Tess is calling me to read a bedtime story to Hannah. Can we talk tomorrow?"

"Sure. Have a good night." Eric ended the call and stared at the star-filled sky just as an owl swooped silently past and landed in a tree. This was the kind of evening he could get used to, especially this mild autumn weather. A bit of tightly held tension released, and his shoulders relaxed. But even now, sleep wasn't going to come easily.

Eric wandered through the downstairs rooms of his huge home. The living room's ornate fireplace was in good shape, but the walls needed fresh paint, some of the baseboards needed replacing and the hardwood floors could stand to be refinished. The list of things that needed some form of repair was long and growing, but he liked a challenge. Using Barton Estate to prove that he knew what he was doing with a historic house meant he'd have proof of his skills. This restoration project would keep his mind and hands busy for months, and it would be the time he needed to regroup and enjoy being out of a big city. And if he was lucky, he'd be tired enough to allow sleep to come easier than it often did.

He peeked in on Lilly and took a moment to watch her sleeping with her tiny hands tucked under her chin, her blond curls fanned out like a halo on the pink pillowcase. This precious child was his everything. "Sweet dreams."

He'd take another look at the original blueprints for Barton Estate and keep his mind from going where it should not.

"I will not seduce Jenny Winslet," he mumbled as he stomped up the stairs where he had the plans spread out. "I will not." He might have to repeat that phrase like counting sheep to fall asleep, and if she slipped into his dreams… Well, that couldn't be helped, but…

He would not seduce the nanny. And he would not allow her to tempt him.

Jenny drove through the sagging entry gate of Barton Estate early the next morning, both eager and nervous about her first day of work with the McKnight family. The long curving driveway was shaded with trees and underbrush encroaching on the rutted surface. Everything was in some state of needing repairs, and it had always been one of her dreams to see the house and grounds restored to their full glory. Maybe Eric would be interested in getting it declared a historic landmark. It did have the accolades of originally being a famous thoroughbred horse ranch, and never having anyone work on the property who wasn't paid for their willing employment.

It made her heart happy that someone was accomplishing what she could not. Around the last curve, the stately, one-hundred-and-seventy-five-year-old house peeked through the arching branches of ancient oaks. As a child, she'd dreamed of one day becoming the lady of this manor. Mrs. Barton had always been so kind, but lonely, reclusive and mysterious. A widow for fifty years with an air of sadness that Jenny had romanticized. A sad tale of lost love and longing. Even though Jenny loved this place, it felt as if its former owner's emotions had seeped into the walls. This stately house was like a broken heart waiting to once again be filled with love and calling out for the joy of a happy family.

The structure needed some TLC, and if her instincts were correct, the new owner could also use some tender loving care. But from what wound she wasn't sure. Her cheeks warmed and it was not from the heater vents. Still, Eric McKnight's care was not part of her job description.

Or was it?

He'd hired her to take care of his child. To make his life easier. So…in a way, his well-being was also part of her job. Giving him the help that he needed. Relieving some of the weight from a single dad's shoulders was the only right thing to do.

Jenny laughed and turned up the Christmas song on the radio, loving that they were already playing the holiday classics. "I sure know how to talk myself into things."

It had always been in her nature to take care of

people, but why did she feel such a need with a man she hardly knew? Her desire to nurture him went beyond the norm and needed to be held in check.

She parked around back near the carriage house, and the golden retriever came running to greet her. "Good morning, Brad." She rubbed his head as he led her to the back door. Before going inside, she cast an eye toward the playhouse in the woods, already envisioning the curtains and pillows she'd make after encouraging Eric to fix it up.

When Jenny knocked and came through the kitchen door, Eric and Lilly were eating oatmeal. "Good morning."

"Fairy girl back," Lilly yelled and clapped.

When Eric smiled at his daughter, his face transformed into one of the most genuine expressions of love Jenny had ever seen. But when he turned to her, his eyes narrowed, and she swallowed hard. His penetrating stare could be interpreted multiple ways. One might suspect judgment, but his mouth wasn't pinched. His full lips were parted as if he'd…whisper her name. Jenny shivered as sparks danced across her skin. If Alexandra and Tess were to be believed, those were bedroom eyes filled with restrained passion. And she wished he'd set it free.

Oh snap. Jenny squeezed her eyes closed. *Stop staring at his mouth and pull yourself together.* Getting tangled up with a guy—particularly her boss—was an epically bad idea, especially right before she was about to *finally* make her move out of Oak Hollow.

"Did you two have a good night?" she asked and ran her fingers through Lilly's curls.

Eric rubbed both hands down his face, as if shuttering his expression. "Yes. Fine. What would you like Lilly to call you?"

"The other kids just call me Jenny."

"Fairy Jenny," the little girl said and bounced in her booster seat.

"That works, too," she said on a laugh.

The second she sat across from Eric, he got up and put his bowl in the sink, as if she pushed him away with some reverse magnetic power. Not very flattering to her ego, and it reaffirmed her suspicion that he didn't want to be near her. But why? Did he feel the same sizzle of attraction that had kept her awake last night?

Or was it just plain old you're-not-my-type?

Discussing the playhouse might have to wait until her new boss could manage to be in the same room with her long enough to have a meaningful conversation. Jenny yanked her thoughts in a safe direction and helped Lilly scoop up her last bite of oatmeal. "I love your cute pajamas."

"Night, night moon." The little girl pointed to the celestial images on her pale blue flannel pj's.

"Do you have the *Goodnight Moon* storybook?"

"It's gone." Lilly held one hand palm up and tipped her head.

"It's her favorite, but we lost it in the move," he said.

"Eric…" His sudden, sharp inhale made Jenny

hesitate. *Hmmm. That's a noteworthy reaction to me saying his name.* But she needed to resist. Didn't she? *I'm doing it again! My self-control is pure rubbish.* "Should I call you Mr. McKnight?"

"No. Eric is fine."

Eric is also totally gorgeous. She almost laughed aloud but somehow managed enough restraint not to embarrass herself. "I called a couple of guys and they're interested in working on this house. Want me to have one of them come over and talk to you?"

"Yes. Have him come out as soon as he can."

"I'll text Chris Lopez. He's become the leader of the group that no longer has a licensed foreman."

"I'm done." Lilly waved her spoon in the air. "Up."

Brad trotted over from his bed in the corner and licked Lilly's toes, making her giggle.

After cleaning his daughter's hands and face with a wet paper towel, Eric lifted her into his arms. "Lilly is just getting over an ear infection and has a few more days of antibiotics."

"So, you've already met Dr. Roth-Hargrove?"

"That wasn't his name, but we saw him before I even had time to unload the U-Haul."

"Oh, that's Dr. Clark. He was supposed to retire when she relocated from Manhattan and joined his practice, but he said he gets bored sitting at home. Did you know he still makes house calls like an old-fashioned country doc?" When his eyes widened, she stopped nervously chattering. "Lilly looks like she's feeling better."

"She's been extra tired and is taking more naps than usual." He adjusted his child in his arms and pointed to a handwritten list on the refrigerator. "Here's her schedule and stuff. Let me know if you have any questions."

Jenny followed him from the kitchen, smiling at Lilly as she peeked over his shoulder. The sun-faded English countryside mural still covered one wall of the dining room. "I know someone who can restore that painting. My friend Alexandra is an excellent artist. She's Dr. Roth-Hargrove's daughter."

"I'll keep that in mind. I don't guess you need a house tour?"

"No. I've searched this house many times. Except for Mrs. Barton's room."

"What were you searching for?"

"As a kid, I heard whispers of secret passageways."

"Really?" He cocked his head and absently patted his child's back as she rested her head on his shoulder.

She'd swear a spark of curiosity lit in his eyes, and it made something swirl in her belly. Maybe this could be something else that helped them form at least some kind of friendship that was less tense than the current vibe sizzling between them. "But I never found any trace of a passageway. It's a miracle I only pulled off one piece of trim while searching for something that would open."

"Hmm." He glanced around the empty dining room.

When Lilly stretched her right arm out to Jenny, she used it as an excuse to move closer and carefully watched Eric's reaction. She wasn't sure whether to laugh or cry when he seemed to hold his breath as she took Lilly from his arms. "Which one is her bedroom?"

"This way." He turned without waiting to see if she'd follow.

Lilly stroked Jenny's long, dark hair. "Pretty."

"Thank you. I wish I had some of your curls."

Eric led her into the room connected to the master. "I'm still working on unpacking."

"I can help with that. Did you know Mrs. B was one hundred and one when she died?"

"No. Did she live here her whole life?"

Jenny untangled the child's fingers from her hair. "She moved in when she married in 1936. She was eighteen years old. Widowed at fifty and never remarried. But she did raise two of her nephews. They are the ones who inherited this house and sold it to you."

"You're like a book of facts." He raised an arm, easily reaching to run a hand along the carved top of the door frame. "I believe this was originally a sitting room for the master, but I like to have Lilly close at night. The other downstairs bedroom is on the other side of the house, and I have stuff stored in there."

"I understand wanting to have her close. Especially in a new house." Lilly wiggled to get down, and Jenny put her on the floor beside an open cardboard box of toys and a small bookshelf that had yet to be filled. "This was considered part of Mrs. Barton's room, so I haven't searched it either. It didn't seem right."

"But it felt right to search the rest of her house?"

Was that judgment in his voice? The gleam in his eyes hinted at teasing, and she relaxed just a bit. "I have boundaries." His lips twisted and she thought he might actually be fighting an urge to smile. "And she knew I searched the other rooms. She'd tell me stories about mysteries and hidden treasures. Fuel for a young girl's active imagination."

"Feel free to search it. *This* room I mean," he added rapidly.

Jenny nodded, understanding he did not want her going into *his* bedroom. "Got it." Once again, that particular room was off-limits.

"Sometimes Lilly scoots on her bottom or crawls rather than walking. I encourage her to use her gait trainer." Eric pulled a small pink four-wheeled walker from the corner. "Let's show Jenny how it works, Lilly Bug." He helped her to her feet and put her hands on the walker.

Lilly started moving around the room with Brad right beside her. "My go-go."

"That's what she calls it," Eric said and leaned against the pale green wallpaper covered with magnolia blossoms. "I should show you how to put on her AFOs."

"What are those?"

"Ankle-foot orthotics." He picked up a small pair of pink-and-white molded plastic braces. "Lilly Bug, let's put these on."

The little girl shook her head. "No, tank you."

"She doesn't like them. I've been trying all kinds of socks for her to wear under them. I need to get thicker socks so they don't press so much on the back of her leg."

Jenny held out a hand for the AFOs and examined them. "Maybe I can make something padded that will help with comfort."

"Really? That would be great. We'll also be getting a larger brace for her left leg after Thanksgiving."

Taking a seat on the foot of the bed, Jenny smoothed the fairy-themed comforter. "Lilly, will you come here and show me how they work?"

She glanced between the adults with the cutest scrunched-up nose and then moved toward her new nanny and sat on the floor. The dog sat behind his little girl and she leaned against him.

Eric grabbed a pair of knee-high socks from one of the boxes, knelt before his daughter and put them on her feet. Jenny held out one of the braces, and when he took it from her and their fingers brushed, he jerked his hand away so fast that it fell to the floor.

"Silly Daddy," Lilly said and giggled.

Jenny covered her mouth to hide her desire to chuckle. This single father was not the confident and cocky ladies' man one might think by looking at him. He was a bit shy and nervous whenever she got near, making her feel not so self-conscious. And his reluctance to acknowledge the attraction she was pretty sure he felt only spurred her to tease him more.

Without a word, he put the brace on her tiny foot. "They go on like this and Velcro in place."

Jenny slipped her finger between the brace and her leg. "I'll try out a few different materials for padding until we get it right. When she's not using her go-go, what about holding her hands and walking with her?"

"That's good, too."

"Lilly and I will work on unpacking and set up her room today." She waved a hand at the stack of boxes that filled one side of the room near a dresser and a pink plastic toy box.

"I'd appreciate that. I'll be working in one of the upstairs bathrooms. Lilly also has a play area set up in the living room."

Jenny rose from the bed and moved closer, and he stepped back so quickly that he whacked his elbow on the door frame before slipping through. It took pressing her teeth hard into her lower lip to keep from laughing. Eric McKnight was proving to be very entertaining. Was it wrong that she was enjoying his discomfort? At least it was helping her not to be so nervous around him.

"Be a good girl, Lilly Bug." He rubbed his elbow as he walked away.

"Bye-bye, Daddy."

Jenny shifted all of her attention to her adorable new friend. “What should we unpack first? How about your clothes?”

“Toys. Not clothes.” Her curls bounced around her face.

Over the next few hours, they put away and arranged toys, books and clothes. Eric checked in on them every few minutes—without getting close enough for actual human contact or conversation. Little did he know that throwing off the brooding tough guy vibe was more tempting than almost anything he could do, making her want to act on her girlfriends’ suggestions. But anything romantic was on the “don’t go there” list. For multiple reasons.

Around noon, Jenny came out of Lilly’s room just as Eric was rounding the corner at the other end of the hall. He changed directions midstride when he saw her coming.

“Eric, wait.”

He paused but didn’t turn around.

“I’m about to give Lilly her lunch. Would you like anything?”

Turning halfway, but not making eye contact, he answered. “No, thanks.”

As she walked away, she caught his reflection in a large hallway mirror, and the gaze he cast her way was…unreadable.

After Lilly ate and they discussed the color of fairy hair and wings, she went down for a nap after one story. Jenny settled the faithful dog with Lilly and left the bedroom door open. Heading toward the kitchen for afternoon coffee, she once again saw Eric coming from the opposite direction. His eyes widened before he veered sharply right, his boots thumping rapidly up the front staircase.

My, my, Mr. McKnight. You make me feel so powerful. Her inner diva purred. A girl had to wonder if Eric was a supernatural creature—like a vampire who was so attracted to her scent that it drove him wild. She laughed softly. "I read too many paranormal romance novels." Jenny made a glass of iced coffee and then pulled out her phone and dialed Tess.

"Was Alexandra right?" her girlfriend said in place of hello. "Is he wild about *and* scared of you at the same time?"

"That's yet to be confirmed. I have a question." Jenny lowered her voice. "What's the story with Lilly's mother?"

"She died when Lilly was an infant."

Eric is a widower. A heaviness filled her chest. Suddenly, some of his behavior made sense. He was mending a broken heart after the death of his wife.

"Jenny, I'm getting another call, and I think it might be the Realtor about my offer on the location for my antiques store."

"No problem. We'll talk later."

She went in search of Eric and found him in the first upstairs bedroom staring at an old set of blueprints. They were pressed between sheets of Plexiglas on a folding table. She raised a fist to knock on the door frame but paused when he put both hands behind his head and stretched, making impressive muscles bulge in all the right places. A shimmery sensation washed over her.

Working for this fantasy-inducing man could be… challenging. On several levels. She'd stick to a strict look-but-no-touch plan. The image got even better when he pulled the elastic band from his hair and let it fall free to graze his shoulders.

Highland warrior, take me away.

Chapter Three

The wooden floor creaked, and Eric turned with a jerk. Jenny stood in the doorway—a beautiful vision backlit by the hallway light. How had she sneaked up on him?

"Lilly is napping. I'm going to the grocery store for my grandmother on the way home and can pick up your list."

"That would be great." Grocery shopping was one of the chores he hated, and this was an offer he wouldn't pass up. "But I don't have a list."

"How about I do a pantry inventory and make one?"

"Works for me." He sneezed into the crook of his arm.

"Are you getting sick?"

"No." When she stepped into the room with a raised hand as if she intended to touch his forehead, he rounded the table. If she touched him, he couldn't be responsible for what he might do. "Just allergies. I took Benadryl."

"I'll add nondrowsy allergy meds to your list. There's probably a tree or something that you're not used to. I bet it's cedar. Any food allergies I should be aware of for either of you?"

As she talked, Jenny trailed her hand along the faded pink wallpaper, coming closer to him with each graceful step. Her floral scent and full lips made concentration impossible, and he scrambled to remember her question.

One corner of her mouth curved up while she waited. "Or any food you absolutely hate?"

Allergies. That was it. "No food or medicine allergies. And no beets. Please," he said, hoping his tan would hide his suddenly warm cheeks.

"Got it, and I totally agree. Pickled beets are the worst."

Thinking she'd go away, he bent his head and got back to work, but she stayed, tempting him like the last slice of apple pie.

"Are these the original house plans?" Her long, thin finger traced along the edge of the plastic protecting the old paper.

Wonder what her fingers would feel like on... Knock it off, fool. "I thought they were, but this room is smaller than it should be."

"Could it be someone didn't follow the plans correctly?"

He shrugged. "Probably has something to do with the two upstairs bathrooms they added in the 1950s."

"They aren't on the plans?"

"No. There wouldn't have been any when this house was built a hundred and seventy-five years ago."

"That's true." Bracing both hands on the table, she leaned forward with a big smile that lit up her face.

"You know, this could mean there's truth to the secret passageway rumor."

He made a noncommittal sound. *Why did I say anything about it?* He'd never thought much about hidden entrances and such, until this woman with the inquisitive hazel-green eyes had brought it up, but now he couldn't get the idea out of his head. Sharing this interest was going to make it that much harder to keep her at a safe distance.

"Remind me to give you cash for groceries." Needing her to leave before he invited her to study the plans with him, he glanced from her to the door.

Taking the hint, she straightened and backed away. "I better go take an inventory of the pantry and make that grocery list before Lilly wakes up."

After taking a minute to pace the room and get himself back in a good head space, he took more measurements of the bedrooms, tiny closets and bathrooms. The numbers revealed that there was indeed space between the walls. But he couldn't find any trace of how to get to it without tearing something out or cutting into a wall. And he didn't want to cause more repair work or mess up original features only to discover it was nothing more than improper framing or some other poor construction.

Saying anything more to Jenny about his discovery and sudden interest in hidden passageways was out of the question. She'd probably follow him around talking endlessly…in her smooth, sexy voice. Driving him up the wall with her enthusiasm. And that was an added temptation he did not need. He was a father and would always put Lilly first, which meant not chasing temporary pleasure.

He spent the rest of the day avoiding the temptress, and once she'd left for the evening and Lilly was in bed, he sat on the porch with a block of aspen wood and his carving tools. Every Christmas he'd made something for Lilly, but he couldn't decide what to carve this year. He began smoothing out the corners and waited for an idea to take shape. Finding this art form had been a life saver for his mental state. And books. They'd always provided the escape he craved, and he read every night.

Jenny hefted the final load of plastic grocery bags and put them on the front porch of the white farmhouse she shared with her grandmother. The one they'd had to take out a second mortgage on when Mimi's medical bills piled up with her first round of cancer treatments. That had been the second time Jenny delayed her plans for design school. And if it hadn't been for the money Mrs. Barton left them in her will, they might've lost the house her grandfather built.

In her usual selfless way, Mimi told Jenny to take half of the money from Mrs. Barton and follow her dreams, but she'd worried Mimi couldn't make the house payment after she left. So, Jenny had gone down to the bank and put most of the money toward paying off the house. Owning it free and clear felt good, and she hadn't minded delaying her plans if it meant the woman who'd always sacrificed her own needs for her girls could relax and enjoy life. Especially now that she was healthy and getting stronger every day.

After going back to close the trunk of her little red Toyota, she paused to admire their home, tucked between two huge ancient oaks and a small grove of fruit trees. Her aunt Nicole—who'd been more like a big sister—used to hold her up to reach the ripe peaches. Mimi would fill three bushel baskets in the time it took the two of them to fill one. She missed Nicole and her niece, Katie, every day since they'd moved to Montana and was sad they wouldn't be home for Christmas this year.

Flashes of childhood memories like this one had been coming more and more. Usually whenever she thought about moving away from Oak Hollow. Something tightened in her chest. *I'm just nervous. And excited.* It was the plan. A bit delayed, but the plan none the less. One that was on the verge of fulfilment.

But would it fill her with happiness like she'd always believed?

A frigid gust of wind made her shiver and rush for the warmth of the house. She squeezed through the front door with her arms loaded and inhaled the delicious aroma of chicken soup. "I'm home."

"Let me help you with that." Mimi rushed over and took some of the load then followed her into the kitchen. "Is there more in the car?"

"It's all on the porch. I need to sort out what's ours and what goes to Lilly and Eric."

Her grandmother gave her the famous Winslet side stare. "He expects you to do his shopping?"

"No. I offered. I was going anyway." She was not going to admit her overwhelming desire to take care of a man she barely knew, especially since he was a puzzle she hadn't solved.

"What's he like?" Mimi asked as they walked outside for the last of the groceries.

"He's a big grumpy bear."

A lock of shoulder-length hair swished across Mimi's cheek when she chuckled. "From that little grin you're trying to hide, I'm betting there's more to this story?"

"His little girl is an angel. Taking care of her will be a pleasure." Lilly was a happy child. So, the man who did his best to avoid his daughter's nanny was doing something right. He was great with his child but being around grown women didn't seem to be one of his strengths. In Jenny's experience, men with his good looks often knew it and were confident with their flirting, but Eric McKnight behaved more like a shy teenager with a crush.

"Jenny? Did you hear me?"

She looked up from the bag of carrots in her hand, not surprised to find Mimi grinning and shaking her head. "I'm sorry. What did you say?"

"I have to finish that dress for Mrs. Suarez tonight. Do you have any sewing you need to do?"

"Yes. I want to try out a few ideas for making something for Lilly to wear under her foot orthotics."

"Surely they make those kinds of things?" Cans and jars clanged as Mimi stacked them on the bottom shelf of the pantry.

"They do. Eric has tried a few different ones, but I thought I'd give it a try and see if I can improve on them."

"I have no doubt that you will." Mimi paused a moment with her hands on her knees before straightening.

"Are you sure you don't need to get some rest? You know what the doctor said. It could take a while to get back to your normal activity level after surgery and your final round of chemo."

"Yes, yes. I know all that." She waved her delicate hand through the air. "I told you that you can stop fussing over me. But for your information, I took a nap this afternoon. That's why I'm not finished with the dress."

Jenny would never stop worrying about Mimi, who usually put her own needs aside for others. "Did Joseph come by today?"

Mimi attempted to hide a grin. "He stopped by for coffee."

People usually mistook Mimi for being a decade younger than her sixty-nine years, and Jenny was glad the handsome widower next door was helping Mimi open her heart again. "I can help you finish the dress, but first I need to eat. That chicken soup smells wonderful."

"I'll fill two bowls while you sort out the groceries for your grumpy bear."

"Mimi, he's not *my* anything. Except for my employer." She ducked behind the cabinet door to hide her blush.

"Does he have family in town?"

"No. He's a military buddy of Chief Curry's." Jenny squeezed the last bag of Eric's into the refrigerator, then stared at the pictures posted on the door. Ones she'd seen every day for years, but today they grabbed her attention. A family photo in front of the house when her niece, Katie, was first born. An older one with her grandparents and Nicole at the beach. Once she moved to New York, Mimi would have no family in town. They'd be spread across the country from Texas to New York to Montana. No longer sharing a home in this cozy little town.

"With all that wool you're gathering over there, I could knit a whole sweater," Mimi said.

She'd been caught lost in thought, again. "Did you talk to Nicole today?"

"Yes. Come eat, and I'll give you all the details."

After dinner, they moved into their sewing room. Shelves of colorful fabrics lined the walls and their sewing machines faced one another so they could chat while working.

Mimi clipped back her gray-streaked hair in preparation for sewing. "You should work on your project. I'm further along on this dress than I thought."

Jenny dug around in one of many clear plastic containers of fabric and pulled out sheer sparkly pieces. "I'm putting these aside. They will be perfect for fairy wings." She put that container away and stepped back to look at the wall of shelves. "Where's that crate of stuff we used to make our new seat cushions?"

"Bottom left."

"I think some of the squishy padding might be what I need for her socks. Actually, until I get it right, I think I'll make them more like leg warmers than socks. This project is probably going to take a bit of trial and error."

Mimi nodded and let Jenny talk, knowing that's how she did her best planning.

With supplies gathered, Jenny got to work and had two versions done in no time, each one covered on the outside with a fun fabric leftover from clothes she'd made for Katie and Hannah. She was so invigorated by the project that she also started on the fairy wings and whipped up an elastic waist tulle skirt for playing dress-up.

"You look very happy making those play clothes. Much more relaxed than when you're fussing with the high-fashion garments."

Jenny opened her mouth to argue but realized she couldn't. This was more fun. And making something for Lilly's enjoyment and comfort was more important than a fancy dress that might be worn only a few times. "I really do like this type of work."

"If you enjoy what you do, it never feels like work."

Mimi often said this, but this time, her statement sank in. While trying to finish one of the *Test Yourself* projects from the list the fashion design school had suggested, it had felt like work. Jenny realized the project was meant to test her skills because the garment would never be comfortable or practical to wear. All the ties, hooks and wraps would make it impossible to undress in a timely manner every trip to the bathroom.

Mimi yawned. "Just a few more stitches and I'll be done."

Even though Jenny was tired and should be in bed, making things for Lilly energized her in a way that made her happy. "I want to make clothes that are beautiful but still comfortable. Clothing made for real life."

"If you want to make clothes for real life, you should consider things like the shirt you made with the flap that tied back for access to my chemo port."

"I've thought about that. Do you think it's still a good idea for me to go away to school?"

"I think whatever makes you the happiest is the right decision."

One of the things she'd miss most was Mimi's company and words of wisdom, and she not only worried about her taking care of herself but also that the cancer might come back. And if it did, Mimi might not tell her because she wouldn't want her to come home and delay her dream again.

Her grandmother wouldn't judge her, but would everyone in town think she'd given up if she never went to school?

Chapter Four

On the morning of their new nanny's second day of work, Eric sat on the front staircase, carefully removing one of the damaged spindles so he could recreate it on his lathe. Getting out to his workshop would give him an escape from the way Jenny appeared out of nowhere—as if she really were a fairy who could materialize without warning. But he also looked forward to working with wood. Building and creating was on the short list of things that relaxed him, and he could really use the calming effect of woodturning about now.

As if his thoughts had conjured her, Jenny appeared on the other side of the stairway banister, right at eye level. And way too close. When her floral scent tickled his nose, he stood and hurried down the stairs with the spindle in his hand. "Need something?" His tone was harsher than he'd intended, and he winced when she shot him a side stare that left him feeling scolded.

"Lilly and I are about to start making lunch. She wants to make a hot cheese and asked for you to eat with her. I just wanted to make sure she's talking about grilled cheese?"

"Yes."

"It should be ready in about fifteen minutes."

He held up the worn stick of wood. "I need to take this out to my workshop." He walked in a wide arc around her and out the kitchen door. He needed time to prepare himself for sharing a meal with Jenny. *Wait.* He stopped in his tracks. She'd told him to come eat lunch as if he was a child she was nannying. He'd have to remind her that it was Lilly she'd been hired to tend. Not him. He could take care of himself and had been doing it the majority of his thirty-five years. His boots ground against the old bricks as he turned, ready to march inside and tell her he would not be called to lunch like a child. But he was hungry. And he didn't want to disappoint his daughter. Eric continued to the carriage house and set up what he'd need to start working on after lunch.

When he opened the kitchen door, Lilly was sitting on the floor beside Brad, playing with a set of wooden blocks.

"Hi, Daddy."

"Hey there, Lilly Bug." He scooped her up, making her giggle when he gently tossed her into the air and then cuddled her close. "Whoa, little fairy. Are you trying to fly away?"

"Fly again, Daddy. Again."

A few more gentle tosses had her laughing, the beautiful sound reducing his stress. He put her in her booster seat. When he turned and met Jenny's eyes, she was smiling in a way that lit her whole face. A way that made him overheat and fight for his next breath. Why did she have to look at him like that—all sunshine and sexiness?

Forcing himself to look away, he grabbed a Coke from the refrigerator and pressed the cold can against his forehead. *I can't let this woman get in my head.* There were too many reasons why getting involved with her was a bad idea. Too bad he couldn't think what any of them were at the moment.

In the center of the kitchen table sat a bowl of fresh fruit salad and a platter of grilled cheese cut into different shapes. There were triangles, squares, diamonds and one star.

Jenny caught him studying the food and shrugged. "I figure why not take every opportunity to teach her something. Today's lesson is shapes. Anson's daughter, Hannah, gave me the idea."

Eric made a sound in the back of his throat that he hoped conveyed approval but glanced away from her smile before he accidentally returned it. He couldn't give her any impression that he wanted to be friends…or more.

Jenny gave Lilly a quick geometry lesson before he was handed a plate with a triangle, two squares and a diamond.

"Lilly, I was just about your age the first time I came to this house. It was Christmas, and I thought it was the most magical place in the world."

"Magic?" Lilly's blue eyes widened.

"Yes. Christmas magic. There were lots of lights

and a collection of snow globes that I thought fairies lived in."

"Christmas fairies?" Her little hands were pressed to her cheeks.

"I think so."

Jenny started a dramatic retelling of some story about being here as a kid, and he concentrated on eating quickly. Getting out of the city was supposed to lessen the constant noise that had assaulted his ears, and it had. Until Jenny Winslet. But Eric couldn't help enjoying their conversation. His daughter's delight was obvious, and hearing Lilly talking and laughing was always a good thing, but he was well practiced at hiding his reaction. If he didn't join in, she'd get the hint and leave him out of the conversation.

As if she'd read his mind, Jenny turned to him, an idea clear in her big eyes. "I realize it's still a week until Thanksgiving, but I can help you get started on decorating for Christmas. Just in the downstairs rooms that you're not working on yet." Her knee bounced rapidly, and she glanced around the kitchen like big plans were forming. "This is a huge house, so I hope you have a lot of decorations. You do, right?"

She was lit up as bright as the Christmas lights she'd no doubt want him to put up outside. His throat tightened, making swallowing and breathing normally a challenge. Her excitement was going to be overwhelming, and he knew she wouldn't like his answer. But at the same time, he couldn't wait to see her reaction. "One box and a three-foot plastic tree."

A chunk of fruit fell off her fork the same moment her mouth dropped open.

Pressing his lips tighter, he barely restrained a smile and the laugh he fought hard to hold back. He hadn't felt like laughing like this in a while, not with anyone other than Lilly.

"One. Box," she said. "Something tells me you've never been voted Mr. Christmas?"

"Nope." He received an immediate narrow-eyed stare that made her full lips pucker into a kissable pout. *God help me.*

"Eric McKnight, are you one of those anti-Christmas people?"

"Not anti. I just don't get the excitement. I never..." He shrugged. "I got the tree for Lilly." He might not understand holiday enthusiasm, but this woman was making him crave a different kind of excitement.

Jenny glanced at the little girl who was busy singing and making a purple grape dance across her plate. "So, you want to give her happy Christmas memories, right?" she continued without waiting for his answer. "What are some of your favorite childhood Christmas memories? The ones you want to pass on to her?"

"Don't have any. Anything is better than most of mine growing up." He didn't like thinking about the bleak holidays in the group home. And he sure wasn't going to tell her about any of it, especially not in front of his daughter. Jenny's features softened, relaying her empathy, but he gave her a hard stare, hoping she'd take the hint and stop asking questions about things he wasn't willing to share.

Jenny cleared her throat and pressed a napkin to her mouth. "Can I… If you'll let me, I'd really love to help you make this a magical holiday season for Lilly."

Her genuinely hopeful expression weakened his resolve, and something knocked against his breastbone. If he agreed to… He had no idea what he'd be agreeing to, but his baby girl deserved all the best. "If I say yes, you're going to go over-the-top, aren't you?"

Jenny's posture stiffened. "What makes you think that?"

"Just a feeling." He wanted to laugh so bad that his throat tingled. "One room." He held up a finger. "You can put a tree in the living room."

"One?" Outrage rang in her tone. "What about the front of the house? It looks magical all done up in lights and bows of greenery and…"

Her words trailed off when he chuckled. "And you wondered why I thought you'd go overboard with the decorating?"

"I'll keep it to a reasonable level of Christmas cheer," she said and added more fruit to Lilly's plate.

"If you'll tell me your plans before executing them, then I guess we can give it a try."

Jenny jumped up from her seat and grabbed a notepad and pen. "I'll start a list."

The gleam in her eyes told him he'd just opened a

can of something he'd probably regret. And her level of "reasonable" likely would not match his. "What kind of list?"

She tapped the pen against her pursed lips. "I think I'll call it Lilly's Christmas List."

Lilly stopped playing and looked at Jenny. "My Christmas?"

"That's right." She turned in her seat to face Eric. "I'm not only going to help you do Christmas right, I'll have you loving it."

He groaned. This sounded like way too much time spent together. And a risk to his sanity and personal space. And he liked a lot of personal space. "Maybe what we already have is enough."

"Daddy, I want a Christmas magic." Lilly spread her arms wide. "A lot and a lot."

Jenny laughed then bit her lip when she caught his stare. *Sorry*, she mouthed. "But I'll make it fun. I promise."

He didn't want her promise. Promises were fragile things that were too easily broken. But what was he supposed to do with the two of them staring at him with hopeful gazes? "Looks like I'll be buying more decorations," he said on a sigh. "If my Lilly Bug wants a big Christmas, I'll make it happen."

His daughter's smile flooded him with love, but when he glanced at the glowing grin of the woman across the table, he momentarily forgot how to breathe. He could not get wrapped up in this acting-like-a-family stuff. He'd made that mistake before.

It won't be that hard to shut these feelings down. But he knew better than that the second the thought passed through his brain.

"First on the list is buying more decorations and getting a bigger tree," Jenny said. "The real ones smell amazing and look gorgeous, but I hate how they just die and get tossed out. Are you okay with an artificial tree? They make some really great ones now."

"Sure." He took a bite of his sandwich. He could probably say nothing, and she'd continue talking and have the entire thing planned without his help.

Lilly clapped. "My tree. My magic tree."

"That's right. Next on the list is baking. Sugar cookies or gingerbread house building?"

Eric looked up to find Jenny staring at him. "Um. You're asking me? You've seen my cooking skills."

"I'll be here to make sure no food burns or catches on fire."

Lilly wagged a finger. "No more yucky stinky food."

His little girl's scolding made the pressure in his chest lighten, and he couldn't resist a chuckle. "Okay, Lilly Bug."

Jenny tipped her head back to the list. "Christmas movie watching. Making wish ornaments."

He wasn't even going to ask what a wish ornament was, because he had a feeling he'd find out, like it or not. He'd just let her write everything down and get it out of her system.

"There's the annual town square Christmas tree contest that everyone comes out for."

A vision of one of those sappy holiday movies ran through his mind. His last—and best—foster mom, Martha Walston, had watched them all the time. "Let me guess," he said in a deadpan voice. "One of those big trees that someone plugs in and everyone cheers like it's the best thing in the world?" *Why am I involving myself in this conversation?*

"No, Mr. Grinch."

Did she just call me a grinch?

"Surprisingly, Oak Hollow does not have a tree lighting. Each business on the square decorates a tree either in their store or on the sidewalk out front. Some people have gotten so into it that it's become an art show. On the same night, there's a cookie contest at the Acorn Café and lots of beautifully decorated houses in the historic district where Anson's family lives. And there's Historic Christmas night with caroling. Oh! Caroling for sure goes on the list."

Eric winced. "I am *not* doing that."

Jenny stopped writing. "Not doing what?"

"Singing. I don't sing."

"But—"

"I. Don't. Sing."

She sighed in overdramatic fashion and went back to her list. "Fine."

He needed out of this room and into the fresh air, where he couldn't smell Jenny's unique scent. Something spicy sweet and sensual that he couldn't name, but it drew him in like a bee to a flower. "I gotta get back to work. Thanks for lunch."

"You're welcome. And you won't be sorry about agreeing to this. I'll finish the list and show you later. I'll tell you all about each event or activity."

No doubt it will be in great detail. Why had he agreed to this Christmas explosion thing? He had a suspicion he'd just handed over control of his household to a woman with more energy than the Energizer Bunny.

Jenny tucked a loose strand of hair behind her ear. "This will be so much fun."

He wasn't so sure about that. After putting his dirty plate in the dishwasher, he kissed the top of Lilly's head. "You two have a good afternoon. I'll be out in the workshop."

Getting my mind off any kind of fun that involves my daughter's nanny.

Eric was just finishing one of the new staircase spindles when Lilly and Nanny Temptation came into view. Jenny was holding his daughter's hands, patiently helping Lilly walk in front of her. He turned off the lathe, dusted sawdust from his shirt, then met Jenny's eyes. "Do you need me?" The second the words left his lips his skin tingled, and he regretted the way he'd voiced his desire.

Is that what I want? A woman to need me?

"I…um…" Jenny stammered as if her thoughts had veered in the same direction.

"Hi, Daddy."

"Hey there, princess." Thank goodness his daughter was there to break the awkward tension that would be difficult to cut even with a reciprocating saw. He stepped close enough to scoop Lilly into his arms and tickled her until she giggled.

"I'm sorry to interrupt your work," Jenny said. "My friend Chris Lopez tried to call you. He's on his way out to discuss working for you."

Eric pulled out his phone and saw the missed call just as a truck pulled up and parked beside Jenny's Toyota. "Guess that's him?"

"Yes."

A tall, lean, dark-haired guy made his way toward them, smiling at Jenny in a way that looked more than friendly.

Lilly wiggled in Eric's arms, waving enthusiastically to the new person in her normal outgoing way.

"Hello, little one," Chris said and waved back.

Eric liked that he'd first acknowledged his daughter before anyone else. He'd give the guy a chance before passing judgment.

Jenny made introductions and the two men shook hands.

When the other man put an arm around Jenny's shoulders and gave her a quick side hug, an unexpected jealousy slapped Eric. His initial reaction was not to hire the guy but having Chris around the house would be a good buffer between him and

Jenny. Something to keep their relationship strictly boss and employee. It was the perfect plan.

A plan that faltered the second Jenny stepped closer and took Lilly from him. Their eyes briefly met, but long enough to add fuel to the spark between them.

"Lilly and I have some books to read before nap time. I'll let you guys talk."

Before she could take more than three steps, Chris stepped into her path. "Are you free for dinner tonight?"

"I..." Glancing between the men, her words faltered. "I have some things I need to do here this evening. Maybe another time."

"You should go," Eric said. "We'll be fine without you." The statement left a bad taste in his mouth.

What the hell is wrong with me? I've known this woman for only a few days. And she's not *a permanent part of our lives.*

She glanced over her shoulder and shot a scowl in Eric's direction. A scowl that only made him want to kiss her until she sighed with pleasure. And maybe a little bit to let the other man know...

Know what? That I'm a dumbass?

"Great. I have something I want to talk to you about," Chris said, obviously thinking the matter was settled. "Does six thirty work for you?"

Jenny shifted Lilly and rubbed her back. "Sure. I'll meet you at the Acorn Café."

"It's a date," Chris said.

Eric was tempted to growl at the other man, but this whole *date* thing had been his doing. He could've said he needed her to be here this evening. He shouldn't have opened his big mouth. And Jenny had looked none too happy about his interference.

She hurried away with Lilly waving over her shoulder and Brad trotting alongside them.

He needed to get used to her walking away, not staying in their lives. Everyone walked away at some point.

Jenny kissed Lilly's forehead, gave Brad a good scratching and left them to nap. At the foot of the stairs, muffled voices drifted from above, and she paused, trying to hear what the guys were saying. She was in a mood with both of them and tempted to throttle Eric for getting in her business.

Now that Chris had returned to Oak Hollow, would he want something more between them like he had in high school? The way he'd acted in front of Eric felt like he was marking her as his territory or some other macho thing. She was not a piece of property to be claimed. Once again, she'd have to remind Chris that friendship was all there was between them.

But what had her the most annoyed was the way Eric had pushed for her to go out with another man. It was evidence that he did not think of her like she did him. All of his moody gazes apparently weren't in line with the fantasy she'd created in her mind.

Off-limits fantasies, Jenny Lynn.

This was good. Anything else would risk her paycheck. And possibly her heart.

With her arms resting on the newel post, she listened to them talk about paint and trim and matching the old tile in the bathroom. When the thump of their boots sounded above, she scooped a lone sock off the floor and headed for the laundry room so she could avoid the awkwardness of having both men stare at her, or her saying something she'd regret.

Once Lilly was up from her afternoon nap, they played and then Jenny helped her practice using her go-go. They found Eric in the kitchen. "Did you hire Chris?"

"Yes." He looked at his watch. "You better get going so you're not late for your date."

"It's not a date. It's dinner with a friend. I've known him most of my life and we've never been more than friends."

"Does he know that?"

She ignored the question and hoped her expression conveyed her thoughts about him interfering in her love life. "There are sandwich makings in the refrigerator." Jenny knelt before Lilly. "I'll see you in the morning."

"You stay here," Lilly said and pointed at the floor.

"I can't, sweetie. But I'll be back before you know it."

"Okay. You be back soon."

"I will." She hugged the sweet child who was stealing her heart. With one last kiss on the top of her head, Jenny grabbed her purse from the counter, but stopped and turned to Eric. "Are you free to go buy decorations tomorrow morning? It's first on the list."

"Me?" he asked and looked around the room like someone was going to jump out and save him. "Why do I have to go?"

"Because it's part of the fun."

"What if I don't think it's fun?"

With his arms crossed over his chest, he reminded her of the stubborn Viking from her current read. She studied his face, looking for a quivering lip or something to tell her he was teasing. *If he's messing with me, he has a good poker face.* She should be totally irritated with his grumpy attitude, but it only spurred her on to make him love Christmas—whether he liked *her* or not. "Who doesn't like having fun? Other than the Grinch. Oh, that reminds me, we need to watch *How the Grinch Stole Christmas.* It's a classic, and movie watching is on the list." She waved at Lilly as she went out the door.

"Bah humbug," Eric called after her.

With her back to him, she allowed herself a big smile. "That's Scrooge, not the Grinch. But thanks for reminding me we need to watch that movie, too."

Don't look back. Do not.

But she did. Eric stood with his hands braced on

each side of the door frame, making his arms look even bigger. And adding fuel and new images to her already active imagination.

The bells above the door jingled as Jenny stepped into the Acorn Café and waved to Sam Hargrove behind the counter. She spotted Chris in a booth. In a black T-shirt and leather jacket, he really was a good-looking guy, fitting the tall, dark and handsome description, and would be the perfect boyfriend or husband. For someone else.

She slid onto the turquoise leather booth on the opposite side. "Hope you haven't been waiting long."

"No. Only a few minutes."

Dawn Hargrove put two mugs of hot chocolate on their table. "Hi, Jenny. How's the new job?"

"It's great. I'll bring the McKnight family in to meet you soon."

"I look forward to it. I'll send my son over to take your order in a few minutes. Timmy said he needs the experience if he's going to take over the family business one day." Her wide smile showed pride in her son.

"Smart kid," Jenny said before the owner walked away, then she wrapped her hands around the warmth of her mug and turned her attention to Chris. "How'd you know I'd want a hot chocolate?"

"Because if it's cold, you order one. Has that changed in the years since I've been gone?"

"Nope. Still true." A sip of the Hargrove family's

special chocolate blend made her taste buds dance. "So, what did you need to talk about?"

He glanced around like someone might overhear him. "Do you know the new nurse practitioner, Dr. Clark's niece?"

"Gwen? Not well, but she seems really nice. Why?" *Please say it's her you want to date and not me.* She ducked her head so she wouldn't give away her thoughts.

"I met her on the side of the road."

Jenny looked up from the marshmallows melting in her mug. "Did you say on the side of the road?"

He took a sip and wiped chocolate from his mouth. "She had a flat and was changing it when I stopped to help, and she was mad as a wet hen. Even banged the tire iron on the ground. She refused my help at first, but after one more try and not being able to get the lug nut loosened, she let me. She paced back and forth the whole time I was changing it. And then…"

"Then what?"

"Then she drove away."

"Christopher Lopez, I know you did not want to meet me here just to tell me you helped someone change a tire."

He rubbed a hand across his short black hair. "I was thinking about asking her out, but I'm not sure if she'll say yes. I just need female advice from a friend who won't judge me."

Jenny almost sighed aloud. This evening was not about him wanting more between them, and she liked that he thought of her as such a friend. "Of course I'll help you. What else do you know about her?"

"She drives a fancy BMW sports car."

Jenny laughed. "You are such a total guy. I was thinking more along the lines of things about her, not her mode of transportation."

He chuckled. "She's beautiful. And educated. And will probably say no to a date with me."

"Why do you think she'll say no?"

"She's a nurse practitioner and older than me. I didn't even finish college after I was injured and lost my track scholarship. I'm a construction worker and she's a professional."

"Chris, anyone would be lucky to go out with you. Are you still working on getting a contractor's license?"

"Yes. And I want to start my own business, or maybe partner with someone else since I don't have a lot of cash."

"See, you're not a deadbeat. You have plans and goals."

"So, you think I should ask her?"

"Absolutely, but I'd wait for a moment when she's not banging a tire iron on the ground."

"Good idea. So, what's up with you and your new boss?"

"Nothing," she said a bit too quickly.

His full laugh made several people turn to look at them. "Liar."

Chapter Five

"Will this take all morning?"

Flashing what she hoped was her sweetest smile, Jenny handed Eric Lilly's adorable purple combat boots. "I could easily make it last all day, but for you, I'll rush things along." Mentioning that she'd planned to take them to the Acorn Café for the Friday lunch special after shopping for a tree and decorations was probably not a great idea. She'd wait and see how the day progressed.

Eric lifted one leg of his daughter's jeans and paused before putting her boot over the brace. "What's this?" He inspected the pastel floral fabric covering the padded sleeve Jenny had finished the night before.

"My new leg warmies, Daddy." Lilly poked it with her finger. "Softie and squishy."

Eric looked over his shoulder. "You made these?"

"I did. Last night I made two pairs, each with a different type of padding. I can't decide what to call them so for now I'll just call them leg warmers."

He stuck a finger between the padding and the

plastic of the AFO. He made a sound that Jenny took to mean approval.

"Those are just prototypes." She moved to stand where she could see if the padding caused any trouble with fitting on Lilly's boots. "I already know a few adjustments I want to make." His features relaxed into the first smile he'd directed her way, and the next breath caught in her chest.

"Thank you for making these for my daughter."

He held her gaze for longer than his normal split second, and Jenny shivered. He wasn't giving off his grumpy-bear attitude, and when both her inner diva and Pollyanna demanded she brush the wavy strands of hair from his forehead, she shoved her hands into the back pockets of her jeans. *Cool it, ladies.* "You're very welcome."

He snapped his head down as if suddenly realizing his mistake. "Would you mind letting Brad outside for a few minutes? I'm going to leave him home today. His paw that had the thorn in it is still bothering him."

"Sure." Jenny opened the door. "Come, Brad."

The dog spun in a circle then ran out the door.

After boots were tied, Brad was inside and everyone was buckled into the double-cab truck—which still had his Chicago business information printed on the door—he drove down the curving driveway and into the section with trees so thick that they created a wooded tunnel.

"In the spring these trees will be covered with

leaves and this section of the driveway is dark. When I was little, I thought it was a tunnel to a magical world." Jenny reached for the radio dial to change the commercial that was playing.

"What are you doing?" Eric asked.

She held up her hands and then put them in her lap. "I was going to show you what station has 24/7 Christmas music. To set the mood for our shopping."

"It's not even Thanksgiving yet. They're already playing Christmas music?"

"Thanksgiving is less than a week away. This year a bunch of us are getting together at Nan's house. That's Anson's grandmother."

"I've met her. And Anson already invited us."

"Oh good. Lilly will have fun with the other kids, especially Hannah."

He glanced back at his daughter, who was happily playing with a doll, and then pulled out onto the farm road.

"And you'll have fun with the big boys," she said. "Hopefully, you'll talk more to them." His side-eyed glance was accompanied by silence, as if to send a message. She sighed and smoothed the emerald velvet lapels of her coat. She'd been told she talked too much when she got nervous, and sometimes even when she wasn't. With a bit of effort, she remained quiet, but the slight quiver at the corner of his mouth was just enough to reveal a glimpse of the humor she suspected he was hiding. But why was he trying to hide a sense of humor?

Eric came to a stop at the junction of two roads. A new sign had been erected at the gate of the old William's ranch. Wildlife Rescue. "Oh my God!"

Eric hit the breaks in the middle of pulling forward, jerking their seat belts into a locked position. "What is it? What's wrong?"

"That." She shook her finger toward the rustic sign. "There's going to be a wildlife rescue on that land."

He sighed and rubbed a big hand across his jaw. "Don't scare a guy like that while he's driving."

"Again, Daddy. Make the truck go bouncy again," Lilly said from the back seat.

"Sorry." She bit her lip. "We've all been worrying that someone was going to build a housing development. I'm just happy to see that it will remain natural."

Still sitting at the stop sign, he squinted at the property and tapped a thumb on the steering wheel. "I really did move to the middle of nowhere."

"Is that a bad thing?"

He shrugged one shoulder. "No. Just different. I'm getting used to it."

She suspected he liked it more than he was willing to admit. He was a very private man who gave away little, except for the love for his daughter that was evident to anyone watching.

Eric looked both ways, waited for a car to pass and then turned toward town. "It's better than I thought it would be."

"It's hard not to love this town. It's a great place to grow up."

"But now that you're grown up, you want to leave?"

"I have a plan, and it's been in place for a long time."

As they drove, she continued to play tour guide, pointing out landmarks and giving him bits of local lore. "That's one of the parks where I played when I was a kid. It's got some nice hiking trails. There's also a little playground on the town square. If it's okay with you, I can take Lilly there sometime?"

"Sure."

He did not seem to be enjoying her attempt to introduce him to his new town, but then she caught a grin and knew he was messing with her. A few blocks from the town square, Jenny pointed to their left. "Turn there and the lumber yard will be up a mile on the right."

"Are we shopping for Christmas stuff at the lumber yard, or are you just trying to get on my good side because you think it's the kind of place I like?"

She chuckled. "They have the best selection of artificial trees and lights. But we'll have to go to a couple of other stores on the square for some of the decorations."

He groaned. "You didn't tell me this would be a multi-store event."

"Let's back up a minute to the 'good side' comment. How'd I get on your bad side?"

He shot her a startled glance. "You're not on my bad side." He pulled into the parking lot and cut the engine. "Let's get this done."

Jenny rolled her eyes. "You make it sound like I brought you here for a root canal."

He started to smile but rubbed a hand over his mouth.

She'd take his almost smile as a small victory. She led them to the Christmas section of the store, with Lilly seated in the shopping cart. "What jumps out at you, Eric? Traditional is the way I would go. The house calls for it."

"If your mind is made up, why are you asking?" he said and tossed a roll of duct tape into the cart.

"I'm polite that way." They turned down the next aisle, and Jenny gasped. "Oh yay, they've added a bunch of new Christmas stuff." She took a strand of shiny red tinsel and draped it around Lilly's shoulders. "What do you like, sweet girl?"

"I like a lot and a lot of sparkle." Lilly pointed to glitter-covered ornaments in red, gold and silver.

"That glitter will get everywhere," Eric mumbled with a groan.

Jenny wanted to laugh but knew better. "Glitter makes everything beautiful. And it vacuums right up."

"No, it doesn't," he grumbled.

While they shopped, she caught Eric smiling at his daughter, love and joy written on his face. But when he looked at Jenny, his expression shifted to the neutral stare she couldn't read.

They left with two shopping cart loads of sparkly ornaments, greenery, lights and a nine-foot tree. Their next stop was the town square. When they made it to the sidewalk in front of the shops along Main Street, Lilly wiggled in her father's arms. "Down please."

He set her on her feet, made sure she had her balance and then took her hand. The little girl reached to take Jenny's hand and they made their way slowly along the sidewalk with Lilly between them. As they neared Mackintosh's Five & Dime, Jenny saw Mrs. Jenkins coming toward them and knew what was about to happen. "Oh shoot."

"What now?" Eric asked, his tone filled with apprehension.

Before she could warn him, one of the town's busiest busybodies waved enthusiastically. "Jenny Lynn, who's your new fella and this sweet little girl?"

"He's not my fella. I'm his daughter's nanny. This is Eric and Lilly McKnight. They're new in town."

The older woman pushed her glasses farther up her nose and made no attempt to hide her inspection. "Hmm. The one who bought the Barton Estate?"

"Yes, ma'am. I'm Eric McKnight."

She raised her brows at Jenny. "And you live there with them?"

"No. I just work during the day. I'm showing them around town."

Mrs. Jenkins opened her mouth to speak but her husband called her name and motioned her over.

Jenny took the opportunity to escape. "See you later, Mrs. Jenkins." She picked Lilly up so they could hurry into the closest store, which happened to be one with women's lingerie near the front.

"Is that kind of thing normal?" Eric asked in a low voice, then his eyes widened at the clothing rack of lacy bras that his hand rested on.

She chuckled at the way he'd pulled his hand away like it had been scalded. "That would be one of our best town gossips. She'll have us planning marriage before nightfall." Eric's mouth dropped open, and alarm hit Jenny. *Why did I say that?* "Don't worry. Everyone knows to take what she says with a grain of salt." Just when he was starting to loosen up, she didn't want gossip to freak him out and frighten him back into his shell.

Lilly leaned in Jenny's arms, grabbed a pair of red silk panties and offered them to her father.

"Put those back, Lilly Bug." He pinched the bridge of his nose. "Why are we in this store?"

"It was the quickest escape route." She peered out the plate glass window. "Looks like it's safe to continue our shopping."

She waved to the grinning woman behind the counter. Jenny hadn't been the only one to notice Eric's discomfort. Some of the tension dropped from his shoulders the second they stepped onto the sidewalk. They made their way to Mackintosh's Five &

Dime, where they bought loads of craft supplies and more decorations.

"I'm hungry," Lilly whined and rested her head on her daddy's shoulder.

"The Acorn Café is just up on the corner. Want to stop there before we go home? To *your* house." Her pulse fluttered in her throat. She couldn't have him thinking she was trying to make it her home.

"I'm hungry, too," he said and rubbed his stomach. "Let's put the rest of this stuff in the truck. Are you sure no one will take the tree out of the back?"

"I'm sure. Plus, we'll be able to see it from the café."

They walked into the café in time to beat the lunch crowd and snagged a booth by the windows. Sam was behind the bakery counter singing along with George Strait's "Amarillo by Morning."

"I forgot to tell you about the singing chef. That's Sam Hargrove. He and his wife, Dawn, own this place."

"You sing, Daddy." Lilly clapped her hands.

"Sorry, Lilly Bug. Daddy does not sing in public."

Jenny almost asked why he hid his amazing voice, but he was a private man. If she was patient, the answer might be revealed in time.

After the ridiculous amount of Christmas decor was unloaded and heaped into a pile in his formal living room, Eric bolted upstairs to work on something. Anything. Jenny's enthusiasm and big cheery smile had been chipping at his willpower all morning. And he was determined not to pull her in to see if she tasted as sweet as she smelled.

At the top of the landing, he paused when Brad barked in a playful way. Jenny's laugh was followed by his child's giggle. His mood lifted as it always did when he heard that sweet sound. There wasn't a lot he could count on, but one thing was for sure, the day his baby decided to make a premature entrance into this world, he'd become the luckiest dad ever. His heart had been hers from the moment he'd reached into the incubator to cradle her teeny-tiny hand and her grip had tightened around his finger. Such a little fighter, and always so happy. Jenny's playfulness brought out the joy in her that much more. His daughter was as drawn to Jenny as he was trying *not* to be.

But Nanny Temptation would leave, and he'd have to find her replacement. He ran his palm along the worn banister, polished to a satin finish from years of touches. He and Jenny both had lives to live far apart from one another. But for Lilly's sake, he was glad Anson had told him to hire Jenny, even if it was only temporary. As for him? He'd suck it up and deal with the way this woman made him feel.

A knot of ice formed in his core and his grip tightened on the banister. *Feel? Oh hell no.* He should not, could not let himself think this way. But he did. In a matter of days this unusual, vibrant woman had made him feel things he rarely—or more like never—experienced.

It's just chemistry. Something that wears off when...

Eric stomped into the hallway bathroom. He wasn't going to revisit those thoughts and was strong enough to ignore something that was bound to fade like it always did. He'd just shove the feelings away and be thankful Lilly could have every minute of happiness while it was possible.

And he'd never ever admit to it, even under threat of torture, but he was especially glad Jenny was teaching him how to do some of this Christmas stuff. For Lilly. He wouldn't be able to ever do it the way Mrs. Christmas did, but he'd give it his best for his kid. Maybe he should be keeping his own list of the things he'd be able to manage on his own next year.

Switching his brain to what needed to be done in this room, he pulled the small leather-bound notepad from his back pocket and flipped to a clean page. The Barton family had added four bathrooms. The downstairs hallway bath dated around 1920, the master bath in the '40s and the two upstairs appeared to have been added in the '50s. But the style felt out of place. He'd make them look more in line with this one-hundred-and-seventy-five-year-old house.

There was a suspicious dark patch on the ceiling above the bathtub, and he needed to get a closer look, but the high ceilings made that impossible without a ladder. The ladder that was in the carriage house.

But if he went downstairs, he took the risk of Mrs. Christmas pulling him into another item on "the list." A man could take only so much in one day.

Instead, he grabbed an old wooden stepladder that had been in the bathroom closet when he bought the house. It creaked under his weight, but he ignored that and the slight quivering shake. When he stretched to run a hand over the spot on the ceiling, the unmistakable sound of old wood cracking reverberated under his boots a second before his world tilted. The fistful of shower curtain was little help in slowing his fall, and because his arm was up, his ribs took the first hit. Then he got his bell rung when the back of his head clipped the edge of the sink. He lay on the cold tile floor, fighting to inhale.

"Son of a bitch," he hissed just as Jenny appeared beside him.

"Oh my God. What happened? I heard the crash and came running."

Heat swept up his neck. This was not the image he wanted to project. He'd learned long ago that women didn't want a weak man. *But I'm* not *trying to impress her.* With an arm wrapped around his throbbing ribs, he gritted his teeth and sat up, fire shooting along his side. "Stepladder broke."

"Let me help you up." She put a hand on the forearm he had wrapped across his torso.

"I can do it." Eric shifted enough to dislodge her soft hand before he gave in to the impulse and did something inappropriate. Using that rickety stepladder had been foolish, and something he'd ordinarily never do, but in his unsuccessful attempt to avoid Mrs. Christmas, he'd lost all judgment. And now it would cost him in embarrassment. "Where's Lilly?"

"Watching a cartoon in the living room. Brad is with her. Eric, I know you said you're fine, but… there's blood trickling down your neck, and the way you're holding your side, you might have broken ribs."

He touched the back of his head and held in a hiss. "It's just a bump. It would be gushing if it needed stitches."

She rolled her eyes and leaned across him to get a better look at his head, her breasts coming dangerously close to his face, and the V-neck of her blue sweater giving him a nice shot of her cleavage.

"I can call an ambulance or take you to the emergency room."

His face felt impossibly hot, and he wasn't sure if it was pain, humiliation or her nearness. The embarrassment of this mistake was a billion times worse because Jenny saw him sprawled like a dead fish on the floor. "No ambulance, and no ER." Testing a deep breath, he rubbed a hand across his side, more concerned about looking like a sissy than anything else. "Nothing's broken."

"How can you tell?"

"Because I've had broken ribs before and know the pain. This isn't it."

The sound she made in the back of her throat told him what she thought about that self-diagnosis.

Gripping the side of the tub, he hauled himself to his feet. She swooped in and pulled one of his arms across her shoulders before he had time to react. "What are you doing?" Needing anyone's help was an uncomfortable feeling. Earlier in life than most, he'd learned self-reliance. "I don't need—"

"Do not even try to argue about me helping you down the stairs. You might not need stitches, although that's yet to be determined, but you've bumped your head and might get dizzy. You don't want to scare your daughter because you take a tumble down the stairs and I'm forced to call the ambulance you don't want."

"Fine," he growled through gritted teeth. They squeezed through the bathroom door and headed for the stairs. "Are all nannies this bossy?" he asked in an effort to take his mind off her fingers splayed on his hip.

"Only when the children are stubborn."

He started to laugh but caught his breath. They made their way slowly down one step at a time, her curvy body rubbing against him with each step.

"Do you have any first-aid supplies? I need to clean that cut on your head and then get a better look at it."

He could feel blood trickling down his neck and soaking into his T-shirt. The cut was in a location that would be difficult for him to tend alone. "In my bathroom. You go check on Lilly, and I'll get the first aid kit and meet you in the kitchen."

"Got it."

After letting his eyes follow the sway of her hips under nicely fitted denim, Eric made his way to the bathroom and leaned against the pedestal sink with a washcloth held against his wounded head. "You are too reckless, McKnight." The initial shock of the fall had rapidly turned into humiliation. He hated not running at 100 percent.

Bad memories of childhood illness made him wince. A group home hadn't been a good place to be weaker than the other guys. He'd been teased for being scrawny and sickly. But one day, he'd grown taller than all of them. Stronger. And braver. There had come a time when they learned to respect him even though he wasn't a fighter, except when he had no other choice.

Why am I letting this woman get in my head?

Years of experience had taught him not to let anyone know when you were vulnerable, and to never give away exactly what you were thinking. And definitely not what you were feeling. Before he could finish his trip down Bad Memory Alley and take the first-aid kit to the kitchen, Jenny crowded into the space that felt way too small for the two of them to be alone in.

"Lilly is still in front of the TV with her head on Brad." She stepped closer. "Let's take off your shirt."

Heat washed across him, but before he could argue, her arms came forward like she intended to hug him. He sidestepped out of reach. "No. I've got it." Having her undress him was out of the question. He took a deep breath, wrangled his shirt off and tossed it into the bathtub. Arms braced on the sink, he prepared himself for whatever she planned to do. Her fingers moved slowly up his neck as she lifted his hair to get a better look. Her touch triggered goose bumps and a shiver he had no control over, and he thought he heard her whimper. Was it because she didn't like the sight of blood, or was she also feeling this thing between them?

"I think you're right about not needing stitches. I can use a butterfly bandage."

The warmth of her breath hit right between his shoulder blades. She was so close, but he couldn't make himself put distance between them, telling himself it was because he needed to stay still so she could tend his wound. But it was so rare that anyone took care of him, he let himself soak it in.

"You're really tall. You must be at least six foot four?"

"Six-five."

She lowered the lid of the toilet and pointed. "Have a seat, please."

At the moment, he didn't have the will to care about her bossiness. He did as he was told so they could get this over with. But when she leaned around him to grab the bottle of hydrogen peroxide, her body pressed against his back, and he held his breath. However long this took would be too long.

Or not long enough.

The warmth of her body so close behind him was making his head swim, and he was shocked that she wasn't talking nonstop. The silence suddenly became too much. "You have a lot of experience with this kind of thing?" he asked.

"I do. I've even taken a wilderness first-aid class."

That surprised him. "You spend a lot of time in the wilderness?" He held in a hiss as she cleaned the cut.

"I like to hike and camp. And it seemed like good knowledge to have."

He couldn't argue with that logic. Once she'd cleaned and bandaged his head, he stood and turned to say thank you just as she stepped forward.

Jenny gasped as her hands flew up to brace against his chest, sparking a flash of heat. Face-to-face they stood frozen, staring and silent. He told himself to step away, but apparently his legs had forgotten how to move.

"So sorry," she said and jerked her hands away.

Backing out the door, he cleared his throat. "No problem."

"You should lie down for a while and see how your ribs feel. I'll help you. Where do you want to go? Your bed?"

"No," he hurried to say. The last thing he needed to do was look up at her pretty face while lying on his bed. "I'm going to the living room with Lilly. And I can get there by myself." When she gave him that female look that said he was being an ass, he knew he'd said that last part with too much force.

"Got it. I'll..." She motioned over her shoulder. "Just go. This way."

To keep from saying anything else, he rubbed a hand across his mouth, closed his eyes and took a breath. By the time he looked up, she was gone. In his bedroom, he put on a clean shirt and thought about getting into bed to marinate in his mortification in private, but that would only add to him looking like a wimp. He could not allow himself to get used to a woman taking care of him. Not again. Still, he had to admit that he'd hired the right nanny. Jenny was a born protector, and at the moment he was thankful for her compassionate—if somewhat bossy—presence.

Eric headed to the living room. Lilly was singing along with a song he'd heard way too many times.

"Hi, Daddy. You watching with me?"

"Yes, I am." He sat beside her on the couch and stroked the top of her head. "Love you, baby girl." After getting into a comfortable position, he closed his eyes.

Eric was dozing on the couch when Dr. Clark showed up.

"Good afternoon, Mr. McKnight. I was in the area

and stopped by to check in on your daughter, but I hear you could use a checkup as well."

Eric jerked his gaze to Jenny, who was leaning casually in the archway. She ducked her chin and slipped out of the room, confirming his suspicion that she'd called the doctor. "I guess it wouldn't hurt." With as much dignity as possible, he pushed himself into a sitting position and faced the kind man who reminded him of his last foster dad, Travis.

"Let's have a look at your head." Dr. Clark made his assessments. "Jenny did a fine job of tending to this cut. Any dizziness?"

"No. None. My ribs took most of the impact."

Jenny peeked around the corner as the doctor lifted his shirt to look at his ribs, a bruise already beginning to form. He didn't dare flinch or react in any way to the poking and prodding. Nanny Temptation bit her lower lip, eyes locked on his bared torso. And when she stroked her fingers slowly across her own neck, his vision wavered, and he wondered if he actually did have a concussion.

Attracting women had never been a problem, but this one was particularly…dangerous.

When she realized she'd been caught, Jenny smiled awkwardly, came all the way into the room and sat on the floor beside Lilly and Brad. "Does he need an X-ray?"

"I do not need an X-ray," Eric snapped.

Dr. Clark covered his chuckle with a cough. "I

don't see any signs of a break. Binding your ribs will help."

"We'll need one of those large stretchy ACE bandages," she said. "And he's almost out of antibiotic ointment. I can run into town and pick up those things."

"Why not use the pharmacy's new delivery service?" Dr. Clark said. "I'll send out everything you need, and it should be here in an hour or so."

With Jenny in the room, Eric was having trouble focusing on what the doctor was saying, but apparently, he didn't need to listen because she'd taken over and seemed to have it handled. He tuned them out and focused on getting his head right. And his libido under control.

The other man held out a hand and they shook. "Don't hesitate to call. Most of the time you'll reach Dr. Roth-Hargrove or my niece, Gwen Clark. She's our nurse practitioner. But I'm still around when they need me."

"Thanks, Dr. Clark."

"I need you to take it easy for the rest of the day and see how your ribs feel in the morning. And call me if you experience any dizziness."

Why did Jenny have to hear that? The moment she walked from the room with the doctor, he stretched out on the couch.

Lilly came over and kissed his cheek. "Daddy needs a nap time?"

"I think I do." He needed the oblivion of sleep to

erase some of the humiliation. He winced when Lilly crawled up to lie beside him.

"I wuv you, Daddy."

"I love you too, baby girl." He tucked his daughter's back against his chest, then fell asleep with her quietly singing along with her movie.

Eric startled awake when Jenny roused him and offered a glass of water and one of Lilly's small plastic cups with two white pills in it.

"Take one now and wait—" The oven timer sounded. "Be right back," Jenny said as she jogged out of the room.

Squinting one eye, he looked at the pills. One Tylenol wasn't going to do it, so he tossed both into his mouth and took a long drink of water.

Lilly was at the coffee table coloring while Brad chewed on a new dog toy. Everything appeared under control. It was a rare occasion when he could let his guard down and know someone else would handle things.

Jenny rushed back into the room. "Dinner is out of the oven." She picked up the plastic cup. "Oh shoot. Did you take both pills?"

"One Tylenol isn't enough."

"It was Vicodin."

He sat forward and winced. "Vicodin? Why'd you give me that?"

"For the..." She swept her hand through the air from his head to his feet. "The discomfort you're obviously feeling. Dr. Clark sent it with all the other stuff."

Tension cramped his gut. "But I won't be able to take care of Lilly."

"That's what I'm here for. I'm staying until you're better. Mimi brought out some of my things while you were sleeping."

Eric stared at Jenny, at a loss for words. It no longer mattered what he wanted because he needed her. "I should've told the doctor that I don't take narcotics."

"Oh no. I thought you said you weren't allergic to anything. I'll call the doctor's office."

He grabbed her hand to stop her from leaving and stiffened when it jerked his ribs. "No. I get bad dreams and sometimes don't remember what happened. I need to get in bed. And stay there for the rest of the night." *So I don't do anything else embarrassing in front of you.*

"Eric, I'm so sorry. This is all my fault."

"It's not your fault. I should've paid more attention to what Dr. Clark said."

Dear God, please don't let me say or do anything I'll regret.

Chapter Six

Jenny brushed baby-soft curls from Lilly's forehead and tucked the blankets under her chin. "Sweet dreams, pretty girl."

A sleeping child was such a lovely sight, she took a moment to appreciate it. The toddler had wanted her daddy to tuck her in, but Jenny's quick thinking had prevented too much crying or the need to wake him. Her story about a fairy living in a red toadstool had the toddler staring wide-eyed until her eyelids fluttered closed.

Brad sat at Jenny's feet looking back and forth between her and the bed.

"Is that where you sleep?" She pointed to the foot of the bed.

The dog jumped onto the mattress, spun once and settled with his nose by the little girl's feet.

"Good night, Brad." She gave the sweet dog a quick scratch on the head.

Standing in front of the closed door to Eric's room, Jenny recalled the look on his face when he realized she'd given him prescription pain pills. This incident was not going to help with the tension between them. She'd probably made things worse. He sure hadn't been happy about her trying to help him, and with his crankiness, she'd been tempted to leave him to take care of himself, but something stopped her. She sensed deep hurt hiding under the surface of his attitude. And she had decided, or rather talked herself into believing, that helping him was part of her job.

Even though she barely knew Eric, she had a strong suspicion that drugging him was the only way to make him rest. Her call to Dr. Clark had eased her fear about harming him, but Eric's claim about how narcotics affected him still worried her.

I should check on him. It's the responsible thing to do.

Once she'd satisfied herself that he was okay, she'd make a bed on the couch. As quietly as the heavy old door would allow, she opened it, paused long enough to make sure his eyes were closed and then move to his bedside. Watching a handsome man sleeping with one massive arm thrown above his head was also a very lovely sight. His chest moved in a steady rhythm under his tight T-shirt, and she breathed a sigh of relief. There was a tiny scar at the corner of his left eye and part of the knotwork tattoo peaked from under his sleeve. The one she'd studied while tending to his head. Too bad he wasn't shirtless like he'd been then. Her breath quickened. Fighting the urge to run her hands across the expanse of his shoulders had been an exercise in restraint.

He sighed in his sleep, and she stepped back. *What am I doing? I'm gawking at my boss while he's sleeping.*

He appeared to be fine. Sleeping peacefully. And she needed to turn around and walk out of his bedroom. Right now. As if her thought caused it, he groaned, thrashed his head and kicked off the blanket.

She froze and even held her breath like that would make her invisible, which of course, it did not. His eyes were open and looking directly at her. This job had become an unexpected adventure and was probably about to come to a very swift end.

"Fairy Jenny." He grinned. "So beautiful."

He's not mad? Heat rose in her core and spread outward. "Thank you." His husky voice did magical things to her body.

He attempted to sit up but hissed and clutched his side.

Before she thought better of it, Jenny sat on his bedside and put a hand on his shoulder, easing him back onto the pillow. "You'll need to move slowly for a few days." She flexed her fingers against the hard planes of muscle and then reluctantly pulled her hand away.

"You'll leave." He squinted one eye. "Just like all the others."

Had all their nannies quit? "I'll be here all night. Lilly is already sleeping, and I'm not going anywhere." But that was a lie. She might not leave them tonight, but early in the new year, she would be across the country. A strange ache started in her belly. The one that had been appearing more and more whenever she talked about leaving Oak Hollow. But it was just her being nervous about such a big change. That's all. And this time it was probably her feeling bad that she'd have to leave Lilly. And her annoyingly grumpy father. Just as she thought he was going back to sleep his eyes sprang open.

"You smell nice." He reached up, his thumb brushing lightly across her lips.

Tingling sensations zipped through her as the breath fled from her lungs, his touch spiking her body temperature.

Eric's fingers trailed across her cheek and then back to her mouth. "Wonder if your lips are really this soft?"

While she was trying to remember how to use words, his hand dropped like he couldn't hold it up a second longer.

"Everyone leaves." His slurred words were almost a whisper.

This was something more than his employees quitting. Wanting to comfort him, she smoothed hair back from his furrowed brow, and he sighed. He had to be talking about his wife's death. She couldn't imagine losing a spouse, and her heart ached for his pain. "Not everyone leaves."

"My parents left before I was Lilly's age. Never came back." He snapped his fingers. "Gone."

Her eyes burned with a need to cry. She'd never known her own parents, but at least she had graves to visit. And her grandmother had been there for her every day of her life. "I'm so sorry. I never knew my parents either. My grandparents raised me."

"Foster kid," he mumbled.

His heavy sigh was filled with so much… Was it loneliness? He hadn't been kidding about how pain meds affected him, because she knew he'd never tell her these things otherwise. This man was a puzzle, but some of the pieces were starting to fall into place. His stoic attitude. His defensive nature. The way he pushed away her help. He needed someone who'd have his back, whether he'd admit it or not. "Eric, take a drink of water and then you can rest."

"Bossy fairy." His lopsided grin revealed a dimple almost hidden in the stubble on his cheek.

She chuckled and held the glass for him while he drank and then put it back on the bedside table.

"You're staying?"

"Yes. I'm staying to take care of you and Lilly."

"*She* didn't. I can understand why she'd leave me but…" He fisted his hand and thumped it against his chest.

The harsh movement and pain in his voice brought a prickly knot to her throat. He was so tough on the outside, but inside beat the heart of a little boy left alone in the world. Not knowing what to say to ease the pain of his mother leaving, Jenny wrapped her hand over his white-knuckled fist, hoping to soothe his distress like she'd done for Mimi during her cancer treatments.

"No such thing as forever." He met her eyes and laced their fingers. "But her own baby? How could she leave Lilly?"

He's talking about Lilly's mother, not his own.

"I might not be worth a forever, but my Lilly Bug is. Should've known better than to marry her. Not again. Won't make that mistake twice. No way." He looked at Jenny, blinking as if he struggled to focus. "I wish she had a mother like you."

Her next heartbeat jolted her whole body. With a tear running down her cheek, she brought their joined hands to her heart. As much as he pushed back, she'd keep trying to help him and ignore his cranky behavior. "You're a wonderful daddy, and Lilly is a lucky little girl." Who was the woman responsible for making him believe he wasn't worth staying with? "Go back to sleep. Lilly is safe and protected. I'll be right here all night."

"Good thing this is a dream," he whispered. "A good dream."

He thinks he's dreaming?

That explained even more about his willingness to share. Jenny remained beside him, still holding his strong but gentle hand, not daring to move until he was in a deep sleep. She wanted to believe there was a man out there who'd someday love her enough to never leave. But this man didn't believe in such things, and apparently never planned to marry again. Eric McKnight was completely devoted to his child. There was no doubt in her mind about that. But would he ever give his heart to a woman again?

Why am I even worrying about this?

Not only was he the man who wrote her paycheck, but the one who—in his lucid mind—didn't want anything to do with her. Eric was wounded in more ways than just his ribs and a bump on the head. He'd been kicked emotionally and was understandably wary of relationships. But he thought she was beautiful, and somewhere under his prickliness, he was attracted to her. Ideas that were way too dangerous took root.

When he'd touched her lips… A shiver rippled through her body, and she pressed her free hand against her mouth, tempted to show him just what she could do with her lips. Even though the temptation was great, she made herself release his relaxed hand and resisted crawling into bed beside him, but the couch was too far away from her patient. She found a blanket and settled into the recliner in the corner near his king-size bed. She'd told him she wouldn't leave and was determined to keep her promise.

By the hazy light of the moon, she glanced around the only room she'd never had the chance to thoroughly search for hidden entrances. A stack of novels sat on the bedside table between her and the sleeping man. Several Westerns, a couple of mysteries, a biography and one that surprised her. An old copy of *Wuthering Heights*. She glanced at Eric and tried to picture him reading the classic.

Military dog tags hung from the lamp and dangled in front of a carved wooden frame. In the photo, Eric's wide smile was almost hidden behind a full beard, and he was looking at the tiny infant cradled in the crook of one arm. Tears spilled from her stinging eyes. *How could anyone leave them?*

His bedside table had revealed new information, but what else could she discover about the mysterious Eric from her spot in his chair? Shadows of a tree branch moved across the front of the fireplace and the empty built-in bookcase. She didn't dare get up to inspect it for a hidden entrance. She couldn't risk waking him. Because if he touched her like that again…she wasn't sure if she could resist.

Eric blinked against the ray of sun beaming directly into his eyes through a crack in the blinds. He turned his head and winced as his injury scraped across the pillow, and he was reminded of his embarrassing fall from a tiny stepladder. A tight knot formed in his belly. He had to start using more of his brain cells around Nanny Temptation. Cautiously rolling to his side, he sucked in a shallow breath and froze at the sight before him.

He blinked rapidly, but the beautiful vision was no dream. Jenny was asleep in his favorite chair with one hand tucked under her chin and her long dark hair trailing over the side, shimmering in the morning sun like black pearls.

What's she doing in here? What happened?

After allowing himself a moment to admire her delicate features relaxed in sleep, he held his breath and used his arm to push himself into a sitting position. The bed creaked and her big hazel-green eyes flew open, and time seemed to freeze. When a slow smile lifted the corners of her full mouth, he wanted to return it, but he could not. Not until he found out why she was in his bedroom. At least she wasn't in his bed. That was a good sign.

Her smile faded in a way that made his chest ache, and he regretted that his indecision and blank expression had alarmed her, but not enough to smile.

"Are you okay?" she asked.

"Why are you in my bedroom?"

She smoothed a hand over her hair and put the recliner into a sitting position. "I wanted to be close enough to hear either of you throughout the night. The living room couch was too far away, and I was worried about the pills I'd given you."

"Did I..."

Her head tilted as she leaned forward. "What?"

"Did we talk last night?"

"Talk?" She looked at her lap and picked at the blanket.

"Yes. As in speak to one another after I took the pills." When she didn't respond or raise her head, tension tightened his stomach. "Did we have a conversation?" He said the words slowly as if that would make her answer.

"Nope. You've been asleep."

He didn't believe her. She was hiding something, but at the moment, he wasn't sure he wanted to know what.

Brad bounded into the room and sat at the edge of the bed. He gave his dog a good scratching. "He's letting me know Lilly is waking up, and he needs to go outside."

"I've got her, and I'll let the dog out." Jenny jumped up, caught her leg in the blanket, hopped on one foot to untangle and then slipped through the open door between their bedrooms. "Come, Brad." The animal scrambled after her.

Eric continued to sit on the side of his bed, straining to remember anything about last night. But nothing came to him. No memories of tormented dreams. No conversations. Had he actually slept peacefully all night long?

Once she returned from letting the dog out, Jenny's and Lilly's happy voices mingled in the next room.

"Did you have nice dreams?"

"I dream Christmas," Lilly said and chattered on about glitter.

After they left his daughter's bedroom, and while no one was around to see him grimace, he got up and stretched, hating that there was still discomfort. He took the extra strength Tylenol he'd thought he was taking yesterday and went to the kitchen to start the coffee. He thought about putting an ice pack on his ribs but feared that would only make Jenny think his injury was worse than it was. She'd hover over him—like a helicopter nanny. And he didn't need the added temptation her nearness brought.

Jenny came into the kitchen with Lilly on her hip just as he took his first sip of black coffee.

"Good morning, Lilly Bug."

"Hi, Daddy."

Jenny brought her close enough for him to give his daughter a kiss. Close enough that he could smell their scents mingle and his head swam. It would be so easy to lean a little closer and give Jenny a kiss, too. He stepped back so fast he banged his heel into the table leg. An image flashed. Jenny's mouth close to his. Her hands on his face. Had his usual narcotic-induced nightmares been replaced by erotic dreams of this unusual woman?

Jenny put Lilly in her booster seat and then pointed from him to an empty chair. "Sit down."

His eyes widened and he crossed his arms over his chest. "You do realize I'm only paying you to nanny one person?"

"Please, have a seat, Mr. McKnight." She amended while trying to hide a smile. "I'm making pancakes."

"She's a bossy fairy," he fake whispered to Lilly and took the chair beside her.

His little girl giggled. "She told me fairy stories for night-night."

"She did? Tell me about it."

While Lilly told him the best parts of the story, Jenny set the table—something he never did—and started cooking, all while humming Christmas songs.

He sipped his coffee, eager for the caffeine to clear the fog from his head. His daughter's sweet voice filled in the tense silence between the adults, and he realized Lilly and Jenny had the same nonstop talking ability. He'd always been the quiet type, listening rather than giving away what he was thinking.

"Which bathroom should I use to take a shower?" Jenny asked and flipped another pancake.

A vision of her with water running over her body made him overheat, and he had to look away before she read his mind. "I guess the one upstairs that I haven't started working on. Or the downstairs hallway bathroom I use to bathe Lilly."

"Okay. Does that long side of your sectional couch fold out into a bed?"

"Yes. Why?"

She hesitated then turned to the stove. "I thought that might be a better option for tonight."

"You're planning to stay again?" Something fluttered in his chest, and he wasn't sure if it was excitement or anxiety. The idea of her sleeping in his house both thrilled and terrified him.

She put a plate of steaming pancakes on the table. "I can tell that your ribs are still bothering you, and I don't want you to make them worse because you have to lift Lilly. Maybe..." Jenny paused with her lip caught between her teeth as she joined them at the table. "Maybe it would be easier if I stay here most nights? Then I wouldn't have the early morning drive and have to fight all that evening traffic."

Eric's head jerked up. "What traffic?"

Jenny grinned and put a pancake on Lilly's plate. "I just wanted to see if you were listening."

Lilly clapped and kicked one leg. "Fairy Jenny stay ever and ever."

Eric's heart hurtled into his throat. He and Nanny Temptation shared a glance; neither of them seeming to know what to say. He had told himself he'd give Lilly every moment of happiness he could, and this woman sure made his daughter happy. So, he would figure out a way to deal with the feelings until she left.

"Lilly, Jenny will only be here for a little while. She can't stay here forever." He took his first bite and wanted to moan aloud. Sweet and fluffy and probably the best pancakes he'd ever put in his mouth.

"Where are you going?" she asked Jenny.

"I'm going to New York City to a school that will teach me more about making clothes. But that's not until after Christmas and New Year's."

Eric added more syrup to his stack. "If you really are planning on staying, I'll pay you extra since today is a weekend. You can use one of the bedrooms upstairs." *Far away from my room.*

Jenny's smile did funny things to his belly, and he couldn't hold her gaze. "There's a bed in the carriage house. I can move it upstairs. But I don't have near enough furniture for this house."

"Few people do. My advice would be to take your time and pick the right furniture. Let the pieces speak to you. Anson's wife, Tess, is in the process of opening her own antiques store on the square. She'll be a great resource. She'll know just the right pieces to make this house come alive."

"Sounds like you want to turn this house into the Beast's castle with all the talking furniture and dishes."

Jenny paused with a bite halfway to her mouth, syrup dripping onto the plate. She chuckled.

"What's so funny?" he asked.

"Just thinking that you remind me of him. Is that why you know so much about *Beauty and the Beast*?"

"Belle?" Lilly clapped. "We watch Belle?"

"I have a little girl." He stated the obvious and could tell from Jenny's expression that she was messing with him. "I've seen it a time or two…thousand."

"I bet. Hey, that would be a fabulous costume idea for Halloween. Lilly could be Belle and you're big enough to make a great Beast."

He wasn't going to tell her that's exactly what had won them first place in a costume contest only a few weeks ago. She did not need to know he had any more holiday spirit than she already did.

"Daddy was Beast. I was Belle. And I won a bi-i-ig ward," Lilly said, giving away her father's secret.

"An award?" Jenny grinned.

The little girl nodded her head so enthusiastically her blond curls danced around her face.

"Do you have any pictures of this?" she asked Eric.

"No." Of course he did, but he didn't feel like sharing them.

"It's cold outside, so it's a good day to check off one of the Christmas movies. Maybe one from the classics section of the list."

His coffee mug clunked on the table as he put it down with too much force. "There are subcategories on this list?"

"There are." Her grin was quick and teasing. "And since you still need to take it easy, we can make our wish ornaments after we clean up from breakfast. It's something my family did when I was a kid."

He didn't even try to argue with her plan.

"More cake, please," Lilly said and tapped her fork on her plate.

"I'm glad you like them." Jenny gave her a second pancake and began cutting it.

"They're really good," Eric said in an effort to be polite.

"Thank you. After I get Lilly set up with some toys, I'll help you bind your ribs."

"I don't need help," he said. That would leave him shirtless with her once again, and he wasn't sure he could handle any alone time this morning.

She rolled her eyes. "You are a difficult patient."

"That's because I don't need a nurse."

"What do you need?"

"No one." *Shoot.* She hadn't asked *who.* She'd asked *what.* "I don't need anything. I've been taking care of myself for a very long time." He stuffed the last bite into his mouth and prayed she'd drop it. "Thanks for cooking. I'm headed for the shower."

After several delay tactics, and spending a few hours in his room, his luck ran out. Brad came to get him, and he followed their dog into the kitchen. The breakfast had been cleared away and the table was covered with newspaper and tons of craft supplies. "Whoa. All of this is for your wishing things?"

"Yes, and you're just in time," Jenny said.

"We make candy," Lilly said and held out the sparkly red and white pipe cleaners she'd twisted and bent into a candy cane.

"That's beautiful, Lilly Bug. Are you going to put it on the tree?"

"Yep." She reached for more supplies and started making another one.

Jenny handed her more red pipe cleaners. "I thought some of this would be good therapy because she has to use both hands."

"It is. Thanks for thinking of that." When she did thoughtful things like this, it was much harder to keep himself from falling for her.

"We waited for you to make our wish ornaments."

Jenny glanced at the oven timer. "Lunch will be ready about the time we finish."

He scanned the array of supplies set out like a craft buffet. "Doesn't look like we'll be eating at this table anytime soon, unless we're using glitter instead of salt and pepper."

Jenny chuckled and handed each of them a clear glass ornament with the top metal cap and wire hanger removed. She put a small funnel in the hole of Lilly's. "Now comes the best part. We get to pick what things to put inside. We have fake snow, glitter of all colors, tiny jewels, sprigs of greenery, red berries and other stuff."

"I want mine and Daddy's the same," Lilly said.

His mood lifted. "Sounds good, baby girl. What do you want to put in first?"

"Snow and glitter!"

Jenny demonstrated how to add the snow then passed a second funnel and the container to Eric. "What color glitter?"

Lilly tilted her head. "Sliver and gold."

They shared a grin at her cute mispronunciation of *silver*.

Once their ornaments were filled with plenty of sparkle and small sprigs of greenery, Jenny held out a strip of red paper. "Write your secret Christmas wish on this." When he didn't immediately take it, she swished it through the air and grinned. "Come on. Don't be scared. Write your wish then roll it up and put it into the glass ball."

Eric took the scrap of paper, his pencil hovering above it, but he couldn't bring himself to write a wish. While Jenny was busy helping Lilly add another dash of glitter, he rolled up the blank paper and poked it into his ornament.

Wishing had never gotten him anything but a one-way ticket to Hurt Town.

Chapter Seven

The sudden tension on Eric's face made Jenny sad, and she wished she could take his hand like she'd done last night. But a sober Eric would not respond with compliments and soft touches.

He squeezed the springy ends of the ornament hanger and fitted them into the hole until they slid into place. "Lilly Bug, what do you want me to write on yours?"

"It's a secret, Daddy." Lilly dropped her voice to a whisper. "Fairy Jenny can do it."

Jenny gave him what she hoped was an *I'm sorry* expression, worried she was stepping on his toes. "I told her fairies know how to keep secrets."

He shrugged. "It's fine."

Lilly wrapped her little arms around Jenny's neck and nestled her face against her ear. "I want you to be my mommy."

Jenny's heart melted into a puddle, and she hugged the sweet child closer. Tears threatened, but she took a deep breath and pushed the emotions down. Little kids said stuff like this all the time, but it didn't usually affect her so strongly. With Lilly seated back beside her, she wrote the little girl's wish and put it in the ornament. She was thankful Lilly had not said her wish aloud in front of Eric.

When it was her turn, she went with the first one that popped into her head.

A family of my own.

Once the ornaments were finished, Jenny started *Beauty and the Beast* for Lilly and was settling in beside her to work on some designs in her sketchbook.

"Fairy Jenny, I want my fluffy, please."

"I'll go get it." Jenny stepped over Brad and headed toward Lilly's bedroom for her favorite blanket, but she froze in place when several very creative curses came through the open doorway of Eric's room. Her first instinct was to tiptoe away, but a tug in her chest stopped her. He had no one to turn to for help. A few steps forward and she saw him struggling with the ACE bandage. She knocked on the door frame and waited for the blank stare she'd undoubtedly get.

And there it was, with an added bit of frustration.

"I know you don't like having me in your room, and you don't need my help, but if you'll let me, it would be easier."

"Fine." He sighed and let the bandage unfurl, one end landing on the floor.

When he squared his shoulders and inhaled, flutters filled her stomach.

Maybe this wasn't a good idea after all.

Bared to the waist of his low-slung jeans, Eric fit

her image of the rugged Highland heroes she loved to read about. Muscles tensed and highlighted by the sun streaming through the windows. Thick wavy hair falling perfectly around his face. She swallowed hard when his eyebrows rose and rushed forward with burning cheeks.

He'd caught her inappropriately staring, and she really hoped he wasn't offended. She had to get a handle on this crush and act like a proper employee. Lifting his arms, he gave her room to walk in a circle as she pulled the bandage tight and smoothed out the folds. This was feeling even more like a historical romance novel where the heroine tended to the wounded warrior. She pressed her teeth hard into her lower lip to keep from giggling and secured the end of the wrap.

"Is that too tight?"

"No. Anson and his family are coming over in a little while."

"Oh good. I want Lilly to meet Hannah. They'll get along well." She clasped her hands together to keep from reaching back out to smooth his binding. His silence said s-o-o much. "I'm going to go now."

Thankfully, she remembered to grab Lilly's blanket on her way back to the living room. A return trip was not on the advised list of activities.

After an hour of avoiding Eric, Jenny answered the front door and was greeted with Hannah's arms wrapped around her legs. "Hello, sweet girl." She scooped her up into a hug. "I've missed you."

"I miss you." She patted Jenny's cheeks.

Jenny smiled at Anson and Tess as they came up the curved front walk. "Why didn't y'all come in around back where you parked?"

"Because Hannah likes to come in through the big fancy doors," Tess said and took her husband's hand as they climbed the porch steps.

"Hannah, I have a new friend for you."

The little girl bounced in her arms. "For me?"

"Yes." She set Hannah on her feet. "Let's go inside and meet her."

Hannah hopped over the threshold and stepped from one knothole to the next but froze when Eric came around the corner. Her little mouth popped open. "Wow! You big man."

Everyone chuckled.

Eric kneeled in front of her. "Now I'm not so big. How are you today?"

"You my new friend?"

The corners of his eyes crinkled as he smiled. "Sure thing, but I bet you'll like playing with my little girl, Lilly, a whole lot more."

"Okay."

Jenny's heart warmed. With his daughter and Hannah, his smile came easy, and he was so much more relaxed and authentic than he was with her. But she knew firsthand that it was easier to be less guarded with kids.

When Eric stood, Tess stepped forward. "It's so nice to finally meet you. Anson's told me a lot about you."

"Most of it bad," Anson said and grinned before Eric could respond.

"You're such a funny guy," Eric said to his buddy. "It's nice to meet you too, Tess. You must be a great woman to put up with him."

"So they tell me." She kissed Anson's cheek.

While the rest of the adults talked, Jenny took Hannah's hand and led her down the hallway. "Lilly, I have someone who wants to meet you."

Lilly used one leg to spin on her bottom to face them. "Hi. Want to play?"

Hannah plopped down beside her new playmate and peered into the dollhouse. "Pretty. We play Barbie?"

Lilly handed her one of the dolls. "You like this one?"

Jenny leaned against the doorjamb and watched the two of them become fast friends. Brad roused from his nap and came over to sniff Hannah. Being an animal lover, Hannah was thrilled to meet a new dog. Jenny chuckled when they draped a pink feather boa around Brad's neck, and he let out a long doggie sigh. The sweet animal glanced her way as if expecting she'd help him out of an embarrassing situation.

Tess came up beside her. "Looks like they've hit it off."

"They sure have. And they have a reluctant but very tolerant dress-up model. Want a cup of coffee?"

"Absolutely." Tess dropped her voice to a whisper as they walked down the hallway. "And I want to hear all about what's been going on here. I heard a rumor that you stayed here last night?"

Jenny wanted so much to tell her friend every detail about when Eric thought he was dreaming, but she could not give away the private things he'd told her. Especially when he didn't even know she knew. The guys were in the kitchen, already eating the chocolate chip cookies she'd set out. "Save some for the little girls," Jenny said teasingly and started a pot of coffee.

Anson kissed his wife. "We'll be outside. I want to see the workshop he set up in the carriage house."

"Take your time," she replied and took a seat.

When Jenny turned from the sink, Eric jerked his gaze away and rushed out the door.

Tess covered her laugh and barely waited until the guys were out of earshot to start asking questions. "So, tell me everything. How have your first few days of work been? Are you getting along with him?"

"There's a bit of tension."

"Sexual tension?" Tess waved a hand. "Never mind. I already know the answer. It's as obvious as the sun at noon."

Jenny gasped. "You can tell? Please don't say it's only from my side and I'm making a huge fool of myself."

Her friend's answer was another laugh. "It's not one-sided. He acts more of a fool than you. I thought I might have to wait until Thanksgiving to see the two of you together, but this is better because there aren't so many people and distractions. You are still coming to Thanksgiving on Thursday, right?"

"Mimi and I are. Eric mentioned they are, too." The coffee had finished brewing and she got up to pour two cups.

"Before they come back inside, tell me more about what's going on. What kind of guy is he?"

"Stubborn and grumpy. Eric is a total alpha male on the outside, but inside..." Jenny sighed, considering how to phrase it. "I believe he tries to keep people at a distance, but I suspect he's as sweet as a Christmas cookie on the inside. The proof is in the way he treats his daughter." It was the whole reason she put up with his abruptness. Well...maybe not the whole reason. She'd thought he was healing from his wife's death, but from what he'd let slip last night, it sounded like the pain was from abandonment. Eric McKnight was...something she shouldn't think about. But he was also funny without knowing it.

"I think I know one of the reasons for his distance. I got the scoop on his wife. Well, as much detail as I could drag out of Anson." Tess rolled her eyes and sipped her coffee. "She decided she wasn't meant to be tied down and took a job in Europe. She expected him to stay in Chicago with Lilly and become a single parent. Eric told her they were either in it together, or they were not. She chose to leave them."

Jenny's throat tightened and she had trouble swallowing the bite of cookie in her mouth. The things he'd said while he thought he was dreaming made more sense now.

Tess sighed. "Your silence is the same as mine. I was also speechless at first. But I'm a little raw about that type of thing since Hannah's birth father left before she was born."

"That's understandable." Jenny rubbed her finger over a chip on the rim of her coffee mug, trying to imagine how deep that must have cut into Eric's already wounded heart.

"I know from experience how scary it can be to open yourself up to anyone again."

"I remember how you fought your attraction to Anson."

"Yeah, it took me a while to get out of my own way and accept love again. Eric is going to be a bit gun-shy. You'll have to give him time."

"Um. No, I don't. I am *not* planning on having any type of relationship with him, other than employer and employee. He can be as shy as he wants." But that was a lie. Jenny was fighting her desire for him every time he was in the room. And even when he wasn't.

Tess didn't even try to hide her grin. "Maybe he needs someone to give him a bit of tender loving care."

"Tess, I need the money this job is providing. I

can't risk screwing that up because he's hot. And driving me to distraction with his brooding tough guy act."

"Perfect. Your favorite type of guy."

"How's the new business venture coming along?" she said as a way of changing the topic of conversation.

"The building for my antiques shop is officially ours," Tess said.

"That's fabulous. Congrats." They clinked coffee mugs with such enthusiasm, coffee sloshed onto the table. Jenny got up for a towel and glanced out the window toward the carriage house. "What is he thinking? He shouldn't be doing that."

"Oh no," Tess said. "What are they doing?"

"I need a workshop like this." Anson turned in a circle to take in the tools neatly hung across the wall and machines lining the center. "You should be proud of the life you've built."

"You can come over and use it anytime," Eric said. His friend's praise meant a lot. He'd worked hard to have a workshop this nice. Worked hard to keep Travis Walston's business alive and growing. Until he'd sold it and left Chicago. But he had to believe that Travis would have wanted this fresh start for him and Lilly.

"Where'd you go on me, McKnight?"

Anson's voice brought him around. "Just thinking about Travis." Eric pulled the tarp off the extra furniture he'd shoved in one corner of the carriage house. "I want to move this dresser and that bed upstairs."

"Why are we moving anything up there? I thought you were keeping it empty until all of the rooms are remodeled?"

Eric hesitated, knowing his buddy would give him a hard time. "Jenny needs a room."

"Oh really? You've decided you need a live-in after all?"

"You weren't wrong about her being good with kids. Lilly likes her. And she cooks."

"And that's all there is to it?" Anson chuckled. "Your appetite? And childcare?"

"What else would there be?" They each lifted one side of the cedar dresser, and the stab of pain across his side made him question his decision to do something this physical.

"You already admitted that you find her attractive. She's single. You're single."

"And she's my employee."

"Temporary employee," Anson reminded him as they walked from the workshop.

"*Temporary* is the key word. Here today and gone tomorrow." Just like most people.

The kitchen door swung open and Jenny rushed out, marching toward them like a soldier on a mission. "Eric, what are you doing lifting that? You'll hurt yourself."

Oh hell no. She did not just do this to me! He gave her a stare that he hoped conveyed displeasure.

Anson attempted to cover his laugh but failed miserably. “Yep. She’s good with children.”

Since she was blocking their path, they set the furniture onto the old bricks of the back patio.

Jenny bit her thumbnail and glanced between them, Anson cracking up and wiping his eyes while Eric looked at the sky. “That didn’t come out right. Sorry. I’m just worried that you’ll—”

“Jenny. I’ve got it handled.” Eric kept his tone controlled, but his message was clear. “Don’t you have something you need to mark off your Christmas list?”

She pulled a face. “Maybe I have something to *add* to the list.” When she spun and walked away, there was a little extra swing in her hips.

Anson’s laughter died down to a chuckle and he braced his hands on the top of the furniture. “Bro, what was that about?”

“I bruised my ribs yesterday. She’s been hovering and trying to nurse me. Is she like this with everyone?”

“No. Just the kids. You must be special.”

“Great.” Adrenalin surged but then settled into a knot beneath his breastbone. He wasn’t special to anyone. Except his daughter.

“Y’all already act like a married couple.” Anson dodged the punch to his shoulder then grinned.

“Do not go there, Curry.”

“Why not? You don’t plan to live the rest of your life alone or as a monk, do you?”

Eric crossed his arms over his chest. "Maybe. I've always been a stick-to-myself-and-don't-get-my-hopes-up kind of guy."

"I get it. I remember how you were when we met in basic training. And I understand the reluctance to open yourself up. Especially with a woman who isn't sticking around," Anson said and then remained quiet, knowing that's what Eric needed.

They sat, one of them on each end of the sturdy cedar dresser, staring in opposite directions, much like they'd done on deployment in Iraq. Layers of dirt crusting their skin. The acrid stench of war. Eric wrinkled his nose in memory then inhaled long and slow, soaking in his new surroundings. It certainly smelled better in Oak Hollow, and he'd quickly grown used to the quiet of the country. Only the rustle of trees and call of birds. An introvert's dream.

The music of his daughter's laugh mingled with that of another child, adding to the peace of his surroundings. "I know Lilly needs a mom, but I don't know how to make that happen."

"One step at a time, my friend." Anson stood and grinned. "Should I get the girls to help me with the rest of the furniture?"

"Shut up and pick up your end." Eric used his legs to lift the furniture and kept his arms close to his body. Did it hurt? Hell yes. But he was well practiced at dealing with pain of all kinds. They hadn't even made it through the door before the women moved in to help them.

"Let us take out the drawers," Tess said. "That way they won't slide out as you go up the stairs."

Eric was about to argue, but with one look and an almost imperceptible shake of the head, Anson warned him to let it go and accept their help. And he had to admit that it was much lighter with the three drawers removed.

With all of them working together, they had the dresser, bed frame and mattress moved upstairs. While Anson held the headboard and Tess held the footboard, Eric bolted on the side rails. He'd made this furniture with intentions of selling it but hadn't had the chance to even try yet.

Jenny used a cloth to dust the fireplace mantle. "This is the room I stayed in whenever I spent the night."

"And let me guess." Eric lifted his head, unable to keep from looking at her. "You searched it for the entrance to a secret passageway?"

"Absolutely. You know I did. One time I accidentally pulled off a piece of molding and had to find a hammer to put it back."

With her hands on her hips, her grin turned into a full-watt smile that shot a jolt right to his heart, and he had to look away. He both enjoyed and hated her being here all at the same time. But having another couple here made her nearness a bit easier to bear.

"What's this about secret entrances?" Tess asked.

"There are rumors about secret passageways in

this house," Anson said, "but I don't think there's any truth to it."

"Bite your tongue, Chief Anson Curry," Jenny said and wagged her finger. "Do not ruin my childhood fantasy."

Anson held up a hand. "I take it back. Ask the history and antiques expert." He nodded toward his wife.

Tess braced her leg against the headboard while Eric tightened the next bolt on the side rail. "In my personal experience, they seem to be pretty rare. I've seen a few, but they were simple and really only a way to get from one room to another more than an actual passageway."

With the last bolt tightened, Eric stood. "You can let go now." Not giving away his growing interest in this subject was wisest, especially if he wanted to avoid spending more time alone with Jenny.

"How was the entrance concealed?" Jenny asked.

"Just latches and then pushing a bookcase. I've heard about people using magnets." Tess ran her hand over the top of the wainscoting that covered the lower half of the wall. "There are strong magnets hidden behind something like this paneling, and then you use an object with another magnet to slide some type of mechanism inside."

Eric dropped the screwdriver into his toolbox. "Like a key?"

"A key? With magnets?" Jenny's eyes narrowed as she drummed her fingers together. "Years ago,

Mrs. Barton gave me a metal star that has a different shaped tip on each point. She said it would open my world to the past and help me discover secrets and solve mysteries. I thought she said those things because I was always reading a Nancy Drew book."

"Is it magnetic?" Eric asked.

"I think it is. I remember it sticking to several things in my bedroom. I can go get it tomorrow."

Jenny shot him a smile that made his heart stutter. "Can I also bring over my sewing machine? It will be easier to adjust and improve what I'm working on for Lilly if I have her and her AFO braces available while I work. I also have ideas for adaptive clothing that gives access to things like medical ports for chemo or G-tube feeding."

Her eyes were bright with excitement, and she'd been so thoughtful with what she'd made for his daughter, there was no way he could refuse. "Sure. Do you know how to make curtains? I need some in my bedroom."

"I noticed that this morn..." Jenny's eyes widened, and she cleared her throat. "Yes. I can make curtains. And I'd be happy to make some for every room in this house." She turned in a slow circle. "This bedroom used to have the most beautiful blue velvet drapes."

"She knows how to make a whole lot more than curtains. Her talent with fabric and thread is amazing and will take her wherever she wants to go." Tess hooked her arm through her husband's. "Let's go get that matching bedside table."

Eric found himself once again alone in a bedroom with Jenny. And there was a bed right behind her. It would be so easy to lay her down and— He rubbed his face, needing that thought to take a long hike.

"I'm sorry about embarrassing you earlier," she whispered. Her hand came forward like she'd touch him, but she crossed her arms and tucked her hands underneath.

Was she having the same impulses? "No worries. I don't embarrass easily." *Liar.*

Chapter Eight

Jenny went to check on the little girls and found them having a tea party. Poor Brad was sitting at the little table looking resigned to his duty in his pink boa. “Are y’all having fun?”

“Yes,” they both said and then started excitedly talking at once.

“Are you hungry? You can come to the kitchen and have some real cookies.”

There were cheers and one bark. Brad rounded the table and stood beside Lilly while she got situated in her go-go. Jenny leaned in to help, and when she stood and stepped back, she collided with something solid, warm and smelling of wood and man.

Eric’s hands gripped her shoulders. “Looks like they’ve hit it off.”

The heat of him so close behind her sent a lovely shiver across her skin. And he wasn’t moving his hands which made it difficult to think and form an answer. “Absolutely. We’re moving the tea party to the kitchen for real snacks.”

After an awkward dance of who would go through the doorway first, Eric insisted she lead with a sweeping motion of his long arm. Rather than running like usual, Hannah walked beside her new friend. Once the kids were seated at the kitchen table with milk and cookies, and Brad had a bone, the adults stood around the island.

Jenny pulled the cork out of a bottle of wine. "Since the girls are having so much fun, would y'all like to stay for dinner? We could order pizza, or I can make something." She paused and wished to recall her words. This was not her house. She cut her eyes toward Eric, but he wasn't glaring or looking the least bit irritable. He hadn't seemed to notice the way she'd invited people to stay longer at *his* home.

"You should stay," Eric said and looked at his watch. "And I vote for ordering pizza in about an hour."

"Sounds good," Anson and Tess said in unison.

While the other three discussed pizza toppings and crust options, Jenny got lost in her thoughts. Even though she'd loved this house for years, she could not let herself settle in like it was hers. And she certainly could not act like Eric and Lilly were her family! No matter how tempting it was.

"Jenny? What do you think?"

She snapped out of her daydream and met Tess's grin. The one that said she had an idea of what was running through her mind. "Sorry. What did you ask me?"

"Do you want peppers on the pizza?"

"Yes. That sounds good."

"Cheese pizza, pease," Hannah said.

"I like cheese," Lilly agreed.

Jenny took a large sip of wine and turned to Eric. "And speaking of cooking, or not cooking in tonight's case, do you think you can build a tall seat or stool that Lilly can safely use to help cook? Something that allows her easy but safe access to the counter."

"Show me what you're thinking, and I can build it."

Hannah spilled her milk and both little girls giggled when Brad rushed over and licked it off the floor.

Tess grabbed the paper towels and began cleaning up the rest. "Are you and Mimi bringing her famous cranberry conserve for Thanksgiving?"

"Yes. Absolutely. She's already started prepping for that and the other dishes she's making. I hope Alexandra's Uncle Sam makes his famous spicy hot chocolate cookies."

"I'm sure he will."

"Sam is the owner of the Acorn Café," Jenny said to Eric. "The one who was singing behind the counter. And that reminds me, we need to think about what cookie recipe to enter in the annual cookie contest on Wednesday night." When his response was his usual unreadable expression, she grinned. "It's on the list. We have to enter."

"*We* do?" Eric asked. "Isn't that something you want to do on your own?"

"Lilly will love the experience. You'll have fun, too." Jenny watched a doubtful expression cross Eric's handsome face, making his full lips cock up on one side.

"Hannah and Anson always help me with our cookie entry," Tess said. "Last year we won third place."

Anson chuckled. "I don't think you're getting out of this one. But it'll be a good way for you to meet some more of the local people."

Eric raised a brow at his friend. "Have you met me? When have I been into meeting a bunch of people, especially in a crowd?"

Jenny rubbed Eric's back, and when she realized what she'd done, she spun away and busied herself at the sink. "Don't worry. Our town is tiny compared to the city you lived in. And the citizens are welcoming and kind. There's so much to love about Oak Hollow. And the holidays are the best. I love this town."

"Then why are you..." Eric paused and shook his head. "Let's get the pizza ordered. I'm already hungry. Anson, do you have a number for the best place?"

"I have the number for the only place that delivers pizza. I'll call."

Jenny tried not to stare at Eric as he and Anson left the room. What had he stopped himself from asking her? She had a feeling it was the same question she was starting to ask herself.

Why was she leaving Oak Hollow?

* * *

Eric waved to Hannah as the Curry family drove away, and then he caught sight of Jenny holding his daughter's hands. They were toe to toe, one in brown suede boots and the other in fuzzy Christmas socks and tiny ankle braces. Lilly tipped her head up and smiled at her nanny like she'd lit the stars. When Jenny returned the adoration, his chest tightened. In a matter of days, the two of them had bonded in a way that would make it so much harder when she left. Before he could pull out his phone to snap a photo, Jenny had lifted Lilly into her arms. The moment was gone. As fleeting as so many good things in life.

Jenny caught him watching and cocked her head. "What is it?"

"It might freeze tonight." *Now I'm talking about the weather?* He wanted to smack his forehead.

"I'll give Lilly her bath so you can rest your ribs after—" she smiled and walked toward the door "—your active day. And thank you by the way. Setting up the bedroom was very thoughtful."

"You're welcome." He rushed ahead of them and held the door.

"I put a bag of Epsom salt by your bathtub just in case you want to soak. They say it helps with soreness."

"Thanks." No need to tell her he didn't like baths. Regular-sized tubs were too small for him to get his whole body under the water at once, and that was not relaxing. But escaping for a shower sounded like a plan he could get behind.

Jenny paused with Lilly on her hip. "We're going to watch one of the shorter Christmas movies before her bedtime. If that's okay?"

"That's fine." He'd be happy just watching them interact and that was a dangerous realization. One that made his blood run hot.

"And you should join us," she called over her shoulder.

He stood in the same spot for several minutes, his jumbled thoughts confusing his senses. With other people around as buffers, he'd had fun and relaxed enough to enjoy Jenny's company. But it was once again just the two of them here to take care of his child. Together. Other nannies had helped him, but it had never felt like they were taking care of Lilly as… partners. Jenny Winslet was different, and it scared the hell out of him.

He'd come here for a new start for himself and his child. Not to complicate things with a relationship that… What? That would be exciting? He shook his head and poured a glass of tea. More likely one that would end in someone getting hurt.

When he heard water running into Lilly's tub, he made his way to the master bathroom. Unwinding the bandage from around his torso felt good but stepping under the spray of hot water was even better. Bless the person who'd invented this showerhead height extender. When it came time to remodel this bathroom, he'd take out this tub/shower combo and put in a large walk-in with two shower heads. Propping his hands against the green-and-black-tile wall, he found he couldn't focus on renovation specifics. Not when his mind was busy trying to make sense of the powerful connection between him and Nanny Temptation. Lust would fade, but if it was more…

He forced away unrealistic ideas and let the hot water beat against his back, loosening muscles he'd tensed to take pressure off his ribs. The bandage washed off the back of his head and landed in the bottom of the tub, but he would not ask Jenny to put on a new one. Self-sufficiency was a must.

Several times he'd wanted to ask why she was leaving Oak Hollow if she loved it so much, but that was none of his business. Who was he to question her plans? Anson had said to take things one step at a time, and he could do that. Taking time to look at every option was always a good idea, especially when inspected from every angle. The "measure twice cut once" carpenter's motto could be applied to other areas of life.

Eric grabbed the soap and lathered his hands. "I need a plan."

He could make it clear they needed to have a strictly professional relationship. But from what he already knew about Jenny, pulling that off would be challenging, if not next to impossible. They could be friends and only friends. That was a doable, if somewhat unappealing plan. And third… He swallowed hard and stuck his head under the spray of water, hoping to wash away any thoughts of taking things to a romantic place.

One step at a time. I can't get ahead of myself. But at the moment he didn't know in which direction to take that first step.

"Step one. Get out of the shower." Eric wrapped a towel around his waist and inspected the bruising on his side. He'd never admit it, but he'd overdone it moving that furniture and was paying the price. He was almost tempted to take one of those pain pills and lose himself in the oblivion of sleep.

After rebinding his torso—all on his own—he dressed in sweatpants and a T-shirt and peeked into the living room to see what he was getting himself into. The fireplace was lit, and classic Christmas music was playing. His child's happy voice mingled with Bing Crosby singing "Jingle Bells." If it were just him and Lilly, he'd sing along. But he didn't sing in front of people.

Lilly wore her favorite flannel pajamas and excitedly used her go-go to walk circles around the room. His heart filled to bursting with love for his child. Her strength and positive attitude made him proud every day. He stepped further into the room, drawn by the homey atmosphere that belonged in a movie and had never been part of his home, except to a lesser degree with his last foster parents, Travis and Martha. The huge pre-lit Christmas tree was up, and he could hear Jenny rustling around behind it.

He smiled at his daughter and sat on the couch to take in the whole holiday explosion. Why couldn't his wife have been like this? "You should've waited for me to help you set up that tree."

She popped her head out from behind the branches. "It was easy. It's just four sections that snap together and boom, Christmas is on its way." She made one more adjustment and stepped into view.

And Eric almost choked on his next inhale. A pair of shiny red pajamas clung to every one of her curves. Hardly any skin was showing, but they were sexy nonetheless. When he'd reluctantly agreed she should stay here, he had not fully considered what it would be like to see her in sleepwear. Silky things that made him want to slide his hand along the curves of her body. He closed his eyes and thought about the steps for how to strip paint from old wood. Anything to redirect his thoughts.

She stood back to observe her work, hands on her silk-covered hips. "We'll let it fluff out a bit on its own and decorate it tomorrow."

When he put a foot on the coffee table, a stack of children's Christmas movies tipped over and two of them fell onto the floor. He picked up a copy of *Frosty the Snowman* and *How the Grinch Stole Christmas*. "Where'd these come from? I don't remember any of us putting these in our shopping cart."

"They're mine." Jenny dropped onto the other end of the couch and curled her arms around her raised knees. "Aren't Christmas songs the best? What other music appeals to people of all ages?"

"You're assuming that I like it." He actually did, but it was more fun to tease her. He was enjoying pushing back against her Christmas cheer and making her work for it.

Her grin slowly turned up at the corners. "Oh, but you will. When I get done with you, you won't be able to resist."

He had a feeling she was right… But not about the music. Jenny didn't take offense at his abrupt nature like some people did. She got that cute little crease between her eyes. Pursed lips that reminded him of a rose bud. And the little growl she occasionally made in the back of her throat when he was being particularly exasperating—on purpose. Eric almost chuckled aloud.

"By the time we finish the list, people will call you Mr. Christmas."

He highly doubted that.

Lilly pushed her gait trainer up against the couch, then with a little help, she climbed up beside him. "Christmas movie, Daddy."

"Which one do you want to watch?"

"Green one."

"The Grinch it is," Jenny said, then jumped up to put the disc into the DVD player. "It's always been one of my favorites. Oh, I forgot the hot chocolate. Be right back."

Lilly snuggled against his side, and he kissed the

top of her head, her curls still damp and smelling of lavender baby shampoo. The opening music began, and his little girl clapped and cheered.

Jenny returned in time to see Lilly's excitement. She looked at the two of them with an expression that struck him square in the chest, as if watching them gave her joy. Momentarily lightheaded, he tipped his head back on the couch.

She set the tray of hot chocolate and snacks on the coffee table and handed him a steaming mug. "I cooled some and put it in a sippy cup for Lilly."

They drank hot chocolate while checking the first Christmas movie off the list. By the time the Grinch's heart had grown, Lilly was sound asleep on his lap. Eric ran his fingers through her soft curls and watched her sleep with one hand tucked under her chin. She was the reason he planned ahead for their future. The reason his heart was full. He glanced at Jenny from the corner of his eye.

Was there room in his heart for another person?

She switched off the TV. "Is it okay if my grandmother comes over tomorrow to make cookies with us? I'm supposed to help Mimi with a new cookie recipe for the contest. And she can bring the star Mrs. B gave me."

"That's fine." With his whole world cradled in his arms, he stood and spoke before Jenny could. "Don't even say it. I can carry a thirty-pound little girl to bed."

"I wasn't going to say a word." She made a zipping motion across her mouth.

When her lips twitched, and he had the urge to kiss her, he knew a strictly professional relationship between them was impossible. That boat had sailed around the time she walked through his door.

"Come, Brad. I'll let you outside."

Their faithful dog stretched and followed him to the kitchen door. Once Lilly was tucked into bed, Eric hesitated at the door of her room. Brad needed to be let back inside, but if Jenny was still up… He shook his head. He could not let her keep him from moving freely around his own house.

When he heard Jenny talking to the dog, he stopped short of going into the kitchen but stepped close enough to peek through the crack between the swinging door and the frame. She pulled a mug of hot water from the microwave and dunked a tea bag. He could go for a whiskey about now. Eric stepped forward but paused. Should he go in and spend more time with her? Alone. At night. Deciding against the drink, he turned to leave.

"Good night, Eric," Jenny called to him.

He winced. "Good night. Come, Brad."

Way to be a big chicken.

Chapter Nine

The crunch of gravel under tires and Brad's bark alerted Jenny of Mimi's arrival. Before she could wash the glitter and glue from Lilly's hands, her grandmother knocked and came in the kitchen door with several large bags of baking ingredients that she put on the table. "Who's ready to make cookies?"

"Me!" Lilly cheered as Jenny set her down beside the dog. "I like cookies."

"Mimi, this is Lilly. And this handsome fellow is Brad."

She tucked her salt-and-pepper hair behind her ear. "Hello, Lilly. I'm so happy to finally meet you." She laughed when Brad held out a paw for a shake. "What a smart boy you are."

"My good boy." Lilly patted her dog's back. "Get Daddy."

As he trotted out of the room, Mimi's eyes followed his retreat. "Is that dog going to get him on command?"

"He is. Brad is an amazing animal." Jenny lifted Lilly and put her in her booster seat. "Let's take a look at what goodies Mimi has brought for us to work with."

"What's goodies?" the little girl asked.

"Things like nuts, chocolate, dried fruit, candy and sprinkles." Jenny pulled out a bag of mini marshmallows. "And these."

"Squishies!" Lilly squealed just as her father came into the kitchen.

"She loves marshmallows." He kissed the top of his little girl's head. "One thing I can make are S'mores." He held out a hand to Mimi. "I'm Eric McKnight. It's a pleasure to meet you, Mrs. Winslet."

She took his hand between both of hers. "You, too. And you just call me Mimi."

Jenny tried to gage his reaction without him knowing. He didn't give her grandmother the same blank expression she often received. It wasn't the same bright smile he gave his daughter, but it was a real smile. As if he was aware of Jenny's assessment, he shot her a sexy one brow arched smirk that never failed to make her inner diva and Pollyanna sigh in unison.

Heaven help me. "So, which recipes are we altering this year?"

Her grandmother arranged the baking supplies as she unpacked them. "I think we should start one batch with a sugar cookie base and another with a chocolate dough. Then we can try different add-ins."

Eric backed away with his hands up. "This is way above my pay grade."

"Nonsense," Mimi said and took him by the arm. "We'll guide you through every step. Today is all about creativity and experimenting with different ingredients. There's no wrong way to do it."

He looked down at the five-foot-two grandmother who still had an arm linked around his. "You didn't hear about the first time I met your granddaughter? There was burning food involved."

"Yucky stinky food," Lilly added helpfully and waved her hand in front of her scrunched-up nose.

He shrugged and one corner of his mouth turned up. "It's true."

Once Jenny was sure she wouldn't laugh, she spoke. "I think between us three girls we can keep the kitchen safe from harm."

"Okay, but you've all been warned."

When all the ingredients, bowls and measuring implements were organized, they started with a lesson in mixing the dry ingredients in one bowl and the wet in another. Lilly was soon wearing more flour than she got into the bowl, but Eric was loosening up and even chuckling. Jenny considered it a win even though they'd have a bigger mess to clean up.

Eric took several balls of each type of dough and made a crater in the center. "Lilly Bug, what should we put in these cookies?"

She patted the ball of dough she'd been playing with. "Squishies."

"Of course. What was I thinking?"

"Daddy, they little tiny squishies."

"These would be hard to roast over a fire." Eric

popped one into his mouth then gave her one with a tickle on her chin. "But they still taste good."

Jenny and Mimi shared a smile. The love between father and daughter was sweeter than any treat they could make.

Lilly helped him fill each cookie with mini marshmallows and sprinkle on crushed pecans. He carefully drew the edges up and over to cover the surprise in the middle.

"Look at you," Mimi said and patted his back. "You got the hang of this in no time. What are you going to call these cookies?"

"What do you think about 'Lilly Bugs'?" He winked at his daughter.

"No, Daddy. Lilly's Squishies."

"Perfect name," Mimi agreed. "You might just have a winner."

Once all the trial run batches were baked and the kitchen was cleaned, they had a tasting to choose their entries. Lilly and Eric decided to enter the chocolate version of their yummy, gooey Lilly's Squishies in the Acorn Café cookie contest. Jenny and Mimi went with sugar cookie stars with candied cranberries and white chocolate drizzle.

By the time all of the snacking was done, Lilly was falling asleep at the table. Eric cleaned her hands and face. "Come on, sweetie, let's get you down for a nap. Thank you Mrs.…Mimi. Please come over anytime." Lilly waved over his massive shoulders as he carried her from the room.

"I like that young man," Mimi said. "Polite and great with his daughter."

"He is good with her."

"And very handsome."

Jenny shrugged and turned to load the dishwasher. "I guess."

"I raised you, young lady. Don't think you can fool me."

"What's that supposed to mean?" She knew but admitting anything aloud would make it too real.

"I'd have to be blindfolded not to see it, and then I'd no doubt feel it. Sizzle, sizzle."

Jenny gasped. "Don't say things like that. Someone might hear you," she whispered and picked up another cookie sheet then dunked it into the soapy water. This made two women who had seen something between her and Eric. Their attraction wasn't just in her head. Apparently, they were displaying it for all the world to see. If he got wind of this, would he freak out? Would he fire her? "I need this job and the money that comes with it."

"I'm glad you took this nanny position," Mimi said.

She was too, but knew this one would be harder to leave than any other. Jenny loved the kids she'd looked after before, especially Hannah and Cody, but there was something about her instant bond with Lilly that tugged extra hard on her heart. And the father? What could she say about him? She didn't know what to say, think or do about Eric McKnight.

"Are you going to wash that cookie sheet until there's nothing left?" Mimi asked.

Jenny rinsed the soap and put it on the drain rack. She'd once again been caught daydreaming. Not much slipped past the woman who'd raised her.

After Mimi left, Jenny hauled her sewing machine, small travel folding table and several totes of fabric upstairs to the spacious bedroom she'd thought she'd never sleep in again. The new furniture was more rustic, and the curtains and paintings were gone, but the comfort of the space remained. In one of the clear containers, she spotted Mrs. B's star resting on a piece of shimmery green fabric. Her pulse rate sped. Could this star and its stories be more than make-believe? Was there truth behind Mrs. B's tales? Was it truly the key to something mysterious that Jenny had felt was in this house all along?

The floor outside her door creaked before Eric appeared in the doorway. "I'm going out to the workshop. Since Brad hasn't learned to come find you upstairs, here's the baby monitor in case Lilly wakes before you come down." He stepped further into the room, set it on the dresser and eyed her pile of stuff with a raised brow.

Jenny's nerves jumped. "I'm not moving in. I promise. Mimi just got a little carried away and brought a lot of stuff because she wasn't sure what I needed." Nervous energy had her blabbering. "Is it okay if I bring one of the kitchen chairs up here when I'm sewing? I'll put it back when I'm done."

"I built a chair that matches this furniture. I'll bring it in from the workshop."

"You built all of this furniture?" She looked from piece to piece then to him.

"Yes."

"Wow, you're really talented. I thought this came from a high-end store." The way he tried to hide his grin made her think of a shy little boy.

"Thanks." He turned to leave.

"Wait. I want to show you the star Mrs. B gave me. The one I think might be more than just decorative." She lifted it from one of the totes by its faded emerald velvet ribbon and held it out to him.

He hesitated before stepping closer but stayed as far away as he could while taking it from her. "It's got Celtic markings on it. Where was she from?"

His wide palm made the star look small, and Jenny had to adjust her focus before speaking. "She was born and raised here, but her husband's from Dumbarton, Scotland. It first belonged to her mother-in-law, so it's quite old."

When his long fingers curled around it and his thumb stroked the knotwork, Jenny's mind went straight to a vision of him touching her just as tenderly. She squeezed her eyes closed and took a breath. "How should we go about this? Just walking around and holding it to every spot in the house will take forever."

Rather than getting close enough to hand it back to her, he put it on the dresser beside the baby monitor. "I guess that's the only place to start until we think of something better."

Like he so often did, he rushed away from her like he couldn't get away fast enough. She sat on the edge of the bed and stared at the spot where he'd been standing. *A place to start. What is this the start of? A friendship? More?*

But how could it be more when she was leaving? She rubbed the spot of tension in the center of her chest, then got up and grabbed the star. Starting at the fireplace, she tested every spot for a magnet. With no luck, she went back to setting up her sewing machine.

The sun had set, and a cold wind whistled around the house. Jenny made two bowls of popcorn. One for stringing with cranberries and the other for eating. She carried them to the living room where the tree waited to be decorated. This was something families did together, and she could not let her heart get too involved. She was helping Eric and Lilly feel the magic of Christmas. But that didn't mean she couldn't enjoy it as well. As she put more wood on the fire, contentment settled over her, and she shivered when the heat hit her chilled skin. Or maybe it was the inner heat Eric awakened. The last few days hadn't felt like work, and she almost felt guilty about taking his money. Almost. But she was counting on it to be able to take the next step in her life.

Her belly tightened at the thought of leaving. It was just nerves, and because she'd been enjoying being in this house that was filled with so many happy memories. That was all it was. Nostalgia and fear of the unknown.

Jenny pushed all of that aside and added another log to the fire. It was time for fun. Playing with Lilly reminded her of her own happy childhood. A smile pulled at her lips. And she was enjoying teasing Eric. The blank stare he'd given her at first had shifted into something more intense but still mysterious. And when she really amped up her Christmas cheer, one of his eyes narrowed and twitched. She was going overboard with her decorating and hitting every tradition, even for her. She chuckled and shifted the logs with a poker.

Still staring into the mesmerizing flames, she took several cleansing breaths. The mantel draped with greenery, crackle of the embers and scent of wood smoke brought on the flash of a Christmas memory. Sneaking downstairs to sleep under the Christmas tree and the strong arms of her granddad scooping her up and tucking her back into bed with a kiss to her forehead. Four holidays they'd had without him now.

Just when she was getting sad, Lilly's happy chatter grew louder, mixing with Eric's deep timbre and creating beautiful music. Why was she more nervous tonight than the day she'd met him? She had first-crush butterflies and zero doubt that it would be hard when she left for New York. With every encounter, he knocked a little harder at her heart. The times he grumbled. The times he smiled or laughed. The times he sent her heart racing with his nearness.

"I'm clean," Lilly announced from way up in her father's arms. Their faithful dog was right behind, tail wagging so hard his whole back end wiggled.

"Good girl. Should we put on some music?"

"Yes. Christmas music." She squeezed her daddy's neck, and he kissed her cheek.

Jenny chose a Nat King Cole CD and then handed Lilly a red glitter-covered ball with a hook attached. "You get to put the first one on the tree."

The little girl was so excited that she shook it and a dusting of glitter sprinkled onto Eric's shirt. He cut his eyes toward Jenny and didn't need to say a word to convey his distaste for glitter.

She didn't try to hide her smile but resisted outright laughter. And had no plans to tell him that he had glitter on his cheek.

Eric walked close enough to the tree for his daughter to hang her ornament. "That looks perfect."

"More, Daddy. You do one."

He put Lilly on her feet and Brad came closer so she could lean on him. Then he chose two more ornaments and they each put them on, his way up high and hers near the bottom.

Jenny snapped several pictures of them for the scrapbook she was making for Eric. She picked up a silver angel and hung it on a branch. "I have an idea. Lilly can decorate the bottom, I'll do the middle and..." She smiled at Eric. "The big guy can decorate the top and hold Lilly up to put on the star."

"Little," Lilly said and tapped her chest. "Middle size and big size." She pointed to each of them in turn and then hugged her dog.

Eric ruffled her curls. "You are so smart."

Jenny moved one box of ornaments to the floor for easy reach and handed them their wish ornaments. "Where are the decorations you brought with you from Chicago?"

"The front closet."

"We should incorporate the traditions you two already started. Want me to go get them?"

"I'll do it." He returned within minutes with a cardboard box and peeled off the packing tape.

Lilly and Brad came over to investigate, and she pulled out a carved wooden dog that looked just like Brad and handed it to Jenny. Then she almost fell into the box as she reached for a wooden angel.

"These are gorgeous." Jenny checked the bottom of one. "Where are they from?"

"I made them," Eric said. "One for each of her Christmases. I'm still working on the one for this year."

"Eric, these are amazing. You really know how to turn wood into art."

He shrugged. "It's just a hobby."

"But you enjoy it? Making furniture and art?"

"Yes. Very much."

"With your talent, it could certainly become more than a hobby if you wanted it to. You could even open a shop on the town square like Tess is about to do."

Lilly returned to sit in front of the tree and was looking up into the branches while whispering to her dog.

Eric grabbed a handful of popcorn, tossed a few pieces into his mouth and made a face. "Did you bring the salt?"

"You're eating the stringing popcorn."

"The what?"

"You know, for stringing on thread to put on the tree."

He stared at the kernels in his hand. "People really do that?"

"People do." She chuckled and handed him the other bowl. "But this one is for eating. It has butter and salt."

He picked up one piece, eyed it suspiciously then ate it. "Much better."

"Daddy, you not helping me." Lilly held up a gold ball and shook another dusting of micro glitter onto her pajamas.

"Here we come," Jenny said, then hummed along with "Silent Night."

"Daddy, you sing now."

He shot a quick glance Jenny's direction. "Not right now, Lilly Bug."

"Da-a-d-dy. Sing."

Jenny hadn't missed the flash of panic in his eyes

and possibly a blush creeping across his handsome face. "We can all sing." The girls started singing, but he did not. "Eric, I know you have a beautiful voice."

"No, I don't."

She laughed. "I heard it with my own ears, and you are really good."

"When?" He froze with an ornament half-hung and his eyes narrowed.

"The first time I came out here to meet you. When you burned your dinner."

"You heard that?"

"At first I thought it was the radio playing, until I saw you." The memory made her smile.

"I don't sing in front of people."

"Don't think of me as 'people.'" She emphasized with air quotes. "And since I've already heard you, there's no reason to be shy now."

He rounded the tree to a spot where he couldn't be seen and remained quiet.

Once the ornaments were hung and a movie was playing, she set Lilly up at the coffee table with sheets of red and green construction paper, glue and the unsalted, unbuttered popcorn. The little girl was seated on the floor in front of the couch with the two of them on either side of her. "Lilly, you can make any design you want. Just squeeze on a dot of glue then stick a piece of popcorn onto the paper."

"This is a good activity to get her using both hands," she whispered to Eric over Lilly's head.

"Yes, it is. Good idea."

"I'm filled with good ideas." She handed him a threaded needle.

"What do you expect me to do with this, other than draw blood when I injure myself?"

She rolled her eyes and picked up her own needle. "You're not going to hurt yourself. If you can use all those tools out in your workshop, you can do this. Watch what I do." She strung three pieces of popcorn and then a fresh cranberry. "I'm making a pattern, but you don't have to. String it however feels right."

Looking skeptical, he grabbed a cranberry and very slowly pushed the needle through. He ate a handful of popcorn from the seasoned bowl and then took a kernel from the other bowl and strung it. He almost immediately poked his finger and hissed.

Jenny gasped before laughing. "Did you do that on purpose just to get out of doing this Christmas activity?"

"No," he growled. "What was that you said about me not injuring myself?"

Before thinking better of it, she took his hand to inspect his finger. He immediately stiffened but didn't pull away, and his fingers twitched when she stroked the center of his palm with her thumb. A tiny drop of red beaded on the tip of one finger. "Poor baby. Should I call Dr. Clark and have him rush right over with his little black bag?" When both of his eyebrows sprang toward his hairline, she feared she'd gone too far with her teasing.

And I'm still holding his hand!

"I think I'll survive." He slid his hand from her grasp and grabbed a napkin from the coffee table.

And to her surprise, he started stringing again. They worked mostly in silence while watching *Rudolph the Red-Nosed Reindeer.*

"When I was little, I would sneak downstairs in the night to sleep in front of the tree," Jenny said.

He tossed a piece of popcorn at her. "Why am I not surprised?"

"Sleeping beside the tree is supposed to help your Christmas wish come true."

"Daddy, we sleep with the tree?"

"You don't want to sleep in your cozy bed?"

"Nope." Lilly crawled closer to the tree and rolled onto her back, staring up into the lit branches. "I stay ri-i-ight here." Brad rolled onto his back to see what she was looking at and barked once before his back end wiggled with excitement.

Both Eric and Jenny grabbed their phones and snapped photos of the pair in an award-worthy shot. "Get in the photo with them," Jenny told him. "I'll get a family photo."

"Do I have to lie on my back, too?"

"That would actually be really cute. It would make a funny Christmas card."

She was shocked when he actually did it. This big man, so gentle with his child, rolled onto his back. Then they sat up for a shot where you could see their smiling faces, Lilly on his lap and Brad with his head on Eric's knee. These were going to be perfect for the gift she was making Eric. A photo journey of this Christmas that would include the list, recipes and memorabilia. Not only a memory but as a map going forward.

An ache started in her chest. She wouldn't be part of their future holiday celebrations. But she would of course come home to spend Christmas with her family, and since Eric and Lilly now lived in Oak Hollow, she could see them, too.

"You in the picture, Jenny," Lilly said and wiggled her finger in a come here motion.

She hesitated for a few seconds but then sat with the dog and child between them and held her camera out for a group selfie. "Say *Christmas*." She reviewed the shot and held it out for them to see. Three smiling faces and a happy pet. One that would be perfect for a family Christmas card…if they were doing that kind of thing.

"I wish we had some of Mrs. B's decorations. I wanted to buy some of them when they had the estate sale, but someone had already bought the whole lot of Christmas decorations before I could get here. Even her snow globe collection." She sighed. "I do have one that she gave me, but I would've loved a few more."

"You like snow globes?" Eric asked as they went back to their popcorn projects.

"I do. Especially old ones with Christmas scenes in them."

"You really do love Christmas."

"And you will, too. I even added it to the bottom of the list. Make Eric love Christmas."

He rubbed his chin villain-style. "You can try… but others have failed."

"Challenge accepted." She stuck out her hand to shake on it, and when he held on a little longer than necessary, her entire body warmed in a flash.

"All done," Lilly announced and turned to look at them on the couch behind her.

When he dropped her hand as if she'd burned him, her inner fire extinguished with a hiss of steam as if doused in water.

"That's beautiful, Lilly Bug. When it dries, we can put it on the refrigerator." A giant yawn stretched his little girl's rosy cheeks, and he lifted her onto the couch between them. "Let's get you tucked into bed."

"Not yet. I need to see my Christmas tree."

"Okay." He held up one hand with fingers splayed. "Five more minutes."

"Then you tuck me in for night-night, and you tuck my Jenny in night-night too, Daddy."

"Then who's going to tuck me in?" he asked and tickled her tummy.

Lilly giggled, fell away from him and put her head on Jenny's lap. "Do daddies need tuck in night-night time?"

"Sometimes they do," Jenny said and shivered as she recalled tucking Eric in after she accidentally drugged him. She glanced his way, but he wouldn't meet her eyes.

The little cutie looked between them then took each of their hands. "Hannah said take turns is nice. You take turns. Tonight, Daddy does tuck in night-night to Fairy Jenny."

Jenny clamped her jaw to keep from laughing at the alarm on his handsome face. *Does he remember me sitting at his bedside?* When Eric rubbed his mouth and stared straight ahead, her amusement faded into desire.

Does he remember caressing my lips like he'd make me his?

Chapter Ten

The huge Christmas tree was decorated with enough glitter to give Eric hives, but his little girl had worn herself out with excitement, making it well worth the months it would take to get rid of every sparkle. A few minutes after climbing onto the couch between them, Lilly had fallen asleep. But not before discussing who needed to be tucked into bed.

He had another flash of Jenny leaning over him, her long hair falling forward and her soft lips under his fingers. Tingles spread up his arms. Being strictly friends was going to be a tough ask. She spiked his attraction meter to an off-the-charts level. When the noise from the TV silenced, he glanced her way. A slow smile curved Jenny's lips as she tilted her head and gazed at the tree, joy clear on her beautiful face.

Flickering flames and strands of multicolored tree lights cast the only light in the room. Added to the crackle of burning wood and soft doggie snores rising from the pup across his feet, the atmosphere had him more relaxed than he'd been in a long time, even with Mrs. Christmas enticing him to let her into his life. And heart.

"Once when I was..." His chest tightened. He'd been about to share a memory. A childhood memory. He never did that. And he shouldn't start now.

"Don't stop." Jenny shifted and tucked her legs beneath her. "Tell me what you were going to say."

"It's nothing."

"I'm a good listener. You can talk to me."

"You talk enough for the both of us." A weight dropped into his belly. "Sorry. I didn't mean that." Hurting her feelings was not at all his goal.

Her brows crinkled, but then she grinned. "You're not the first person to tell me I talk too much, but you hardly talk at all. What do I have to do to get you to tell me anything about yourself? Slip you another Vicodin?" Her eyes rounded right before she tilted her head and let her hair screen her face.

Prickly goose bumps spread across his skin. "What's that supposed to mean?" He had a bad feeling he already knew but hoped she'd tell him his fears were unfounded.

"Nothing." She sighed and then continued, "You could just stand to chill is all."

"Jenny Winslet, what did I say to you while I was out of it?"

She lifted her head. "You mentioned that you were in foster care."

"And?" He could tell there was more she wasn't saying. He held her gaze, willing her to speak.

"I would've been in foster care too if it weren't

for my grandparents." Her hands clenched, and then she rubbed her palms along her thighs.

"You're trying to change the subject."

Lilly stretched and mumbled in her sleep, and Jenny rubbed her little back. "And you did that. You said things I couldn't understand."

He hoped that was the truth. But tonight, too many emotions were hovering at the surface. Digging further into this event could wait. "I better put this one in bed." Shifting Lilly into his arms, he stood. "Good night."

"Sleep well, Eric."

He highly doubted he'd sleep well. Not with her constantly testing his will with her charms.

Brad roused and followed him into Lilly's bedroom. Eric tucked her under the covers, kissed her forehead and her eyes popped open.

Her little mouth twitched into a smile. "I like Christmas wishes, Daddy." She rolled onto her side, tucked up her legs and drifted into dreamland.

A rush of emotion clogged his throat and tears stung the backs of his eyes. Was he enough for his child, or was it time to open himself up and give her a female role model? There were things he couldn't teach her. Things he knew nothing about.

"My little girl deserves a mother." He would put himself on the line over and over for his child, but Jenny wasn't the most sensible choice—as their home addresses would soon enough demonstrate.

Why hadn't anyone told his heart?

* * *

Jenny continued to sit on the couch long after Eric retreated from the room. Her inner diva pouted about his rejection while Pollyanna cried for his pain, and she agreed with both of them.

Once again being in this house had her emotions extra exposed and sensitive, but knowing that Eric and Lilly were making it a loving family home made her happy. Barton Estate would once again see Christmases and birthdays. And maybe… Would he ever let her in enough to see if they could have something real between them? Even if it was only friendship?

Using what she now knew about him, her bull in a china shop method needed to be adjusted. Tomorrow she would follow his lead and back off. He'd never said those words, but she suspected that's what he wanted. And if that's what he needed, she'd give him space before she said anything more and revealed that she knew some of his secrets.

I should take the hint and follow his lead.

She was here to do a job, not fall for him and his adorable child. When the fire died down enough to leave it, she unplugged the tree lights and made her way up the stairs with nothing but moonlight as her guide. She shivered as she slid between the cool sheets. It sure would be nice to have a warm body to snuggle up against.

With a sigh, she lifted Mrs. Barton's star from the bedside table. They'd been so busy that she'd hardly done any searching for magnets in the walls. She traded the star for her sketchbook, turned on the bedside lamp and started working on another idea for adaptive clothing while the details were still fresh in her mind. She'd seen a photo of the new leg brace Lilly would get soon, and she wanted to make a pair of wrap pants that went over the brace and allowed easy access to adjust it. The ideas flowed, and she continued sketching until late into the night.

Something cold and wet touched her hand and she sat up with a start. Brad was at her bedside, with his sweet face propped on the edge of the mattress, looking at her with such patience. "Good morning, sweet boy." She rubbed his soft fur, stretched and climbed out of her warm bed. "Let's go see what everyone else is doing."

The dog hurried down the stairs ahead of her. Eric's deep voice reached her before she made it to the bottom step, and she listened to the two of them talking about Santa Claus, then joined them in the kitchen. She stopped short at the sight of Eric standing at the stove stirring what smelled like oatmeal. Sweatpants hung low on his hips and his fitted black T-shirt showed off every muscle. "Good morning."

"Morning," he said without looking at her.

"I'm so sorry I overslept. I was working on some design ideas and stayed up too late, and I forgot to set an alarm."

"No problem."

Lilly raised her arms and Jenny picked her up from her spot on the floor beside her set of blocks. "What would you like to do today?"

The little girl hugged Jenny's neck and kissed her cheek. "Play and books."

"That sounds like a wonderful plan." If only she could once again feel the simple pleasure of being a child. Deciding what to play and not having any major life decisions hanging over your head. Her grandparents had given her a beautiful childhood, but the quiet man standing at the stove had probably never had that uncomplicated peace, and it broke her heart. He'd no doubt grown up way too fast, mostly alone in this world. She wanted to wrap her arms around him and hug him like she was doing with Lilly, but she had promised herself she would back off and give him the space he wanted.

"Oatmeal is ready," Eric said and filled a bowl for Lilly.

While they ate, she couldn't miss his lack of eye contact and the hesitancy hovering between them. "What do you have planned for the day?" she asked him.

"More demo upstairs, then I have some things to do in my workshop."

She almost joked about him not climbing any ladders but held her tongue. Eric McKnight was not in a playful mood this morning. She reminded herself yet again that she'd decided to give him space.

But that space was filled with desire and so many possibilities. Like the potential for a passionate relationship.

Eric spent most of the day avoiding Jenny. Not because he didn't want to be around her. Quite the opposite. He wanted to take part in Jenny's list of Christmas activities, or whatever Nanny Temptation and Lilly were doing. He was putting off setting the boundaries between them, because he didn't know where to set them. So, avoidance won the day. And surprisingly, she didn't push him on any of it. She didn't even call him in from his workshop at lunchtime. Maybe he'd finally done a good job of keeping her at a distance.

Too good. Because her sudden change of attitude did not feel like a victory. And he was more confused than ever about what he wanted to happen—or not—between them.

While reading in his recliner before bed, he remembered that today would've been Travis's birthday. He got up, poured a whiskey and went out onto the front porch where a cold breeze lifted his hair. "Cheers, old man." Eric tapped his glass twice on the porch railing, lifted it toward the sky and then took a long drink. The familiar burn slid down his throat and warmed his belly. The porch swing squeaked, and he jerked his head to the darkened corner. Jenny was wrapped in a blanket, swinging slowly, with moonlight shadows dancing across her cheek. So much in her element, like she belonged in this place.

"Sorry to startle you," she said. "I thought you saw me when you stepped out. Who's the old man you're thinking about?"

He hesitated but discovered he wanted to talk about Travis and celebrate his life. "My last foster dad. Today would've been his ninetieth birthday." The tough, big-hearted man who could've had him put in jail but took him under his wing instead. The person responsible for him being a decent human being and a successful businessman.

"Tell me about him."

He moved closer to the swing and leaned against one of the large white columns. The night sounds wrapped around them and the air smelled fresh and clean. "I started living with him and his wife, Martha, when I was fourteen. They were an older couple, and she died a few years later. Except for the years when I was in the Marines, I stayed and worked with him until he passed away." With his tongue loosened by whiskey, he continued, "He's the one who taught me everything I know about construction."

Rather than the destruction I was bent on causing.

It had been in his pain of losing Travis that he'd let his guard down, forgotten his rules and let his wife, Cilia, into his heart, and they'd been pregnant and married before he realized his mistake. They had been as suited as oil and water. Then in a knife-twisting jab, she'd decided she wanted her freedom more than a family. A familiar and unpleasant sensation cramped his gut. Even years later, the shock and anger of the day she walked away still simmered inside him. And the guilt. Because he'd tried to tell Cilia what to do, Lilly didn't have a mother.

Eric tossed back the remainder of his drink. That painful bit of history was a reminder that he needed to be cautious and take his time when it came to matters of the heart. It was too late to keep Jenny firmly in the employee zone. Working on her Christmas list had seen to that. He'd never had a close female friend, but he could give it a try.

Why do I have to put a label on what's between us? I could just let fate take over.

"Sounds like Travis and Martha became your family."

Her voice pulled him from spiraling thoughts. "The only one I've ever had. There's something about being raised by an older generation that gives you a different perspective."

"I get that. I was raised by my grandparents. How old were you when you went into the foster system?"

"Two."

"What happened to your parents?" Jenny motioned to the spot on the swing beside her, offering him a place to sit. "Please tell me to shut up if I'm overstepping."

He hesitated but then sat on the opposite side of the swing. "They left me with a babysitter and went on a weekend trip. And never came back. Why were you raised by your grandparents?"

"My mom left college and her boyfriend and came home pregnant. After I was born, she called him. He showed up in Oak Hollow with a ring and asked her to marry him. But they never got the chance. They died in a motorcycle accident a few weeks later." A cold gust of wind lifted her hair to dance around her head.

"I'm sorry." He put his arm across the back of the swing and smoothed down her hair before he realized what he was doing, but it felt right.

She smiled and sighed. "At least I have a photo of me with both of them. And I've had a beautiful life. My grandparents raised me alongside my aunt Nicole who was ten years younger than my mom. Nicole recently moved to Montana with her husband and daughter, Katie. I miss them so much."

"Will they be home for Christmas?"

"Not this year. They can't afford it after their big move." She let out a long breath. "Mimi hasn't said anything, but I know she's sad that it won't be our usual family Christmas."

"You and Mimi could spend it with us." His muscles tensed. He'd surprised himself with the offer. But friends could spend holidays together. Right?

Her smile came quick and easy. "That would be nice. It's always fun to have a little one around on Christmas morning. Mrs. B would be happy to see a family Christmas in this house once again."

He couldn't stop himself from staring when she looked out into the night. With silvery moonlight on her face, she was breathtaking and mysterious. His shiver was not from the cold weather on this peaceful night.

He wouldn't be able to ignore her again tomorrow. One day had been enough of that.

Chapter Eleven

Two days later, Jenny had given up on backing off or ignoring Eric. Their time together on the front porch had cut through the tension, and they'd parted that night with what felt like the beginning of something good. What exactly that was remained to be seen. He was a man whose life had thrown him some major curves, and he'd built thick protective barriers. A slow and gentle approach was the way to move forward.

After a morning walk with Lilly and Brad, Jenny followed the two of them into the library. Eric sat at an antique dark wood desk—the only piece of furniture in the large room—working on his computer. Most of the built-in shelves were empty except for an area where he'd started unpacking a stack of boxes with *books* handwritten across the sides. A bottom shelf was set up with a few children's books and small toys. She liked the way he'd set up little areas for his daughter in all the rooms where he spent time. He was a wonderful father, and it made her wonder what hers would've been like.

"Hi, Daddy."

"Hey, Lilly Bug. What are you doing?"

"I'm walking and walking." The wheels of her go-go bumped softly over the old floorboards as she and her dog made a circle around the desk, then stopped at her area to play. Brad nuzzled her cheek then ambled over to lie across Eric's feet.

Jenny and Eric shared a smile. "Some comfy chairs would be good in front of that fireplace." She ignored her phone chiming from her back pocket.

"Good idea. And a rug. It echoes in here." He tapped his hand on the desktop in demonstration.

"Well, at least your desk is perfect for this room."

"It belonged to Travis."

Her phone continued to chime like she was the most popular person in town.

"Someone sure wants to get ahold of you," he said and stretched his arms above his head.

To keep from looking at the way the muscles of his arms and chest flexed, she pulled the phone from her pocket and glanced at the screen. Every member of Queen Mothers was texting her with some version of the same message. They wanted her to meet them at the shop so they could discuss something. She chuckled. "I'm being summoned by the Queen Mothers."

His eyes widened. "That sounds official. Does Oak Hollow have royalty or is that code for something?"

"That depends on who you ask. It's a group of ladies who have been sewing together for many years.

Anson's grandmother and mine are members. They meet every week in a back room at the fabric store, Queen's Sew 'n' Sew."

"Do you think something is wrong?"

"No. All the texts read more like they're plotting something." She adored these lively ladies who had taught her so much over the years. There was no telling what had them so worked up today. "Guess I should stop by and see what words of wisdom they have to share. I do have a few errands I need to run. I can take Lilly with me so you can work."

"She can stay here if you want to get your errands done faster. I'm planning to work on house plans and ordering supplies on the computer most of the day. I'll need some things for when the guys start work in a couple of weeks."

"Can I bring you anything from town?"

"Just y— Um." His forehead crinkled as he scratched his head. "I can't think of anything."

Was he about to say, just you?

"I'll be back soon." She turned away and rubbed her forehead. *No. That's just wishful thinking.*

Jenny opened the front door of the blue-and-white Craftsman house with the big sign that read Queen's Sew 'n' Sew. People came from all over the Texas Hill Country to shop at this unique fabric store. She'd been lucky to have it so close to home, both as a place to work and shop. She waved to Barbara behind the register and made her way through two rooms of fabric collections. The whir of sewing machines reached her before she entered the back room. “Good morning, ladies.”

A round of cheery hellos greeted her, and several of the women started talking at once. Mimi smiled and winked at her, and Nan, Anson’s grandmother and leader of this lively troop, waved her over.

“Come look at this.” Nan turned the open laptop so Jenny could see the screen. “That designer, Loren Lane, is doing an open call for design submissions. They’re looking for new talent and might even give someone their own line. It opens next week, and we want you to send them some of your original creations.”

Jenny took the empty seat beside Nan and looked at the computer. A little thrill tickled her belly. “They’re probably only taking submissions from established fashion designers with experience and a degree, which I don’t have, yet.”

“It doesn’t say anything about a degree being necessary,” Nan said. “Looks like they are searching for fresh talent, just like you.”

“And you do have experience,” Mimi said. “How many paying customers have you had over the years?”

“A lot.”

Mrs. Grant reached around her sewing machine and patted Jenny’s hand. “And do you have a label you put in all of your clothes?”

"I do." She'd sewn her Creations by Jenny label in every original garment she designed.

"They'd be lucky to have you," another lady said. "And we'd all be happy to have you stay closer to home. We're a little worried about you being alone in that big city."

It wasn't the first time she'd heard this sentiment uttered by one of her small town's well-meaning residents. And she wasn't about to admit that being so far away from everything she knew scared her, too. "Does it say where the Loren Lane offices are based?"

"Dallas," the whole group said in almost perfect unison.

Jenny chuckled. "That's also a big city."

"Are you going to do it?" Mrs. Grant asked.

Jenny smiled at their eager faces, beaming with so much hope and excitement. "Sure. Why not? It's worth a shot."

"I should call them and tell them to snap you up," Nan said.

"I don't think they'll listen to any of us," Mimi said. "But Jenny's designs will speak for themselves."

Her heart gave a little leap. But she couldn't allow her hopes to get too big. Getting a job at Loren Lane and staying closer to home was tempting, but what about the plan? The one she'd been saving money for. She needed to make sure this whole open call thing was legit and not some scheme for the fashion house to get their hands on her designs for little or no money. She'd have to read all the fine print before sending them anything.

"Thank you all for telling me about this. I'll look it all over this evening."

Once Jenny was lovingly dismissed by the Queen Mothers, she picked up a few items from her house, stopped by the pharmacy to print photos for Eric's scrapbook and bought more Christmas stuff. She couldn't resist a miniature tree and set of tool ornaments for Eric's desk. He'd originally said she could decorate one room, but she'd blown that plan out of the water. Lilly's bedroom was Christmas fairy themed, and even the kitchen had swags of greenery with sparkly ornaments across the tops of the windows. What would he do if she added a few decorations to his bedroom? It was a room she really wanted to get into. For multiple reasons.

When Jenny's car rounded the thicket of trees that blocked his front gate, Eric felt something suspiciously close to butterflies. She smiled and waved before driving past to park by the carriage house. He'd never been this happy about the arrival of an employee.

That's because she's more than an employee, bonehead.

He tossed the ball to Brad who retrieved it and dropped it in front of Lilly where she sat on the raked-up pile of leaves. She patted her dog's head then rolled the ball to her daddy just as Jenny jogged around the corner.

"My Fairy Jenny back," Lilly announced loud enough to startle a bird from the pecan tree.

Brad ran over to greet her with enthusiastic tail wags, and a nose against her cheek when she kneeled beside him.

Eric had the urge to do the exact same thing, minus the tail wagging. "Brad, fetch." Eric tossed the ball. "So, what was the royal emergency?"

"They want me to submit some of my designs to the Loren Lane fashion house."

"Come see." Lilly swished her hands through the leaves.

Jenny sat beside her, lifted Lilly onto her lap and cuddled her much like Eric often did. "They're holding an open call and are accepting design submissions from amateur designers."

"Amateur?" Gears clicked into place and started turning in his mind. Maybe she wouldn't need to go to school. "Does that mean you don't have to have a degree to work for them?"

"I looked over the application, which the Queens mostly filled out for me, and it says no degree necessary. There's also a place to list accomplishments and experience and stuff like that. But I haven't read all the fine print yet. Sounds like they want to train in-house, which probably means starting at the bottom and working your way up."

"Where is this business?"

"Headquarters are in Dallas. About four hours from here."

He did not like the way he was getting all "hopeful" about her staying closer to Oak Hollow. "Are you going to send them something?"

"I am. It certainly can't hurt. Can I use your computer to look into it a bit more?"

"Sure." When Lilly lay her head on Jenny's arm, he glanced at his watch. "I think it's nap time for a tired little girl."

"I have a few things in my car to unload and then I can get her settled."

"Tell me you didn't buy more Christmas stuff," he said with a grin, so she'd know he was teasing.

"Um… Maybe."

The way she cut her eyes toward him and gazed up through thick lashes made her look like a shy fairy. He held out his arms to take Lilly, then once she was settled on his hip, he offered his free hand and pulled Jenny to her feet. When her fingers squeezed his palm, their gazes connected, and they paused for several heartbeats. His skin tingled, and he kept her hand in his as they made their way to his front door. The woman beside him was unusually quiet, and if her fluttering pulse was any indication, she liked holding his hand.

He reluctantly released his hold to go through the doorway. "Why don't you unload your car and I'll get Lilly out of these dirty clothes and into bed?"

"Okay." She looked both ways like she couldn't

decide which way to go, then went back out the front door.

He chuckled. At least he wasn't the only one who was having trouble focusing and acting like an adult.

Eric turned on his laptop and connected to the internet. When Jenny found him in the library, he stood and motioned to the chair. "It's ready for you to use."

"Thanks." She slid onto his leather chair and started typing.

He stretched his back and tried to decide whether to stay or give her privacy.

"Looks like I'll have to send sketches as well as sample garments. I wonder what designs I should send? It has to be something that stands out and makes an impression." She drummed her fingers on the desk then went back to typing with a big grin on her face.

Her excitement made him happy, but he couldn't just stand there watching her. "I'll be in the attic checking a few things."

"Alright," she said but kept typing.

Eric worked cautiously to pull out the first of two dusty antique doors that were wedged behind the framing in a corner of the attic, hoping he could refinish them for use in one of his restoration jobs. Pulling out the second door revealed an ornate wooden trunk with a rounded top and a metal band with a lock that was cold against his fingers. He wiped a thick layer of dust from an engraved oval that read *Barton*. Jenny would be thrilled with this find. He carried it down the stairs and into the living room. She was on the sofa drawing a dress in her sketchbook. A fire crackled, and the cozy scene allowed his breath to come easier.

"Look what I found in a corner of the attic." Eric placed the trunk on the floor beside the coffee table.

"Oh wow." She put aside her drawing. "How did no one else find this?"

"It was hidden behind some old doors."

She reached for the trunk, then pulled her hand back. "What's in it?"

"Well, it's too small to be a body, and not heavy enough to be gold."

She laughed. "That sure narrows it down."

"I didn't want to open it without you. I don't guess you've seen any old keys small enough that they might open this lock?"

"I'm afraid not."

"Be right back." He went to his room and grabbed his lock-picking set from the back of his sock drawer. He'd been hoping he wouldn't have to break this skill out in front of her. Back in the living room, he got to work.

"You know how to pick a lock?" she asked from over his shoulder.

"Yep." He could feel the heat of her behind him and had a strong urge to lean just enough to feel her against him.

"Where'd you acquire that skill?"

He paused and glanced over his shoulder. "On the streets of Chicago. I lived a few places where no one paid much attention to me sneaking out at night. And getting into trouble." He held his breath and waited for her to back away, or her eyes to shadow like so many did when learning about his past. But she grinned, and he sighed inwardly.

"Your skill is coming in very handy. That was before you started living with Travis and Martha?"

"Yes. Before." Once he turned back to his work, the lock was open in a few seconds, and he moved aside. "Want to do the honors?"

"Absolutely." Jenny reached for the lid but clasped her hands against her chest. "I wonder what's in here?"

"You have to open it to find out," he said and surprised himself with a short laugh. The sound must've surprised her too, because she looked at him with wide eyes then an even wider smile.

"You have a nice laugh. You should use it more often. And your singing voice, too."

He made a zipping then locking motion across his mouth and pretended to toss a key over his shoulder.

Jenny rolled her eyes before pulling the trunk closer to the couch. The lid creaked as it moved on dried-out hinges, opening for the first time in who knew how many years. Nestled in red velvet sat a colorful assortment of Christmas decorations.

"Oh my green goddess. It's Christmas stuff." Jenny clapped her hands rapidly in front of her chin.

The action reminded him of Lilly clapping when she got excited. Something inside his chest shifted. He rubbed his breastbone and sat beside Jenny. "The perfect treasure for Mrs. Christmas. And don't think I didn't notice the tree on my desk."

She leaned her shoulder against his. "And you love it. I'm so glad you found this trunk. I couldn't have thought of anything more perfect to put on the list. Discover hidden antique Christmas ornaments." She opened a faded green box to reveal a glass ornament with the hand-painted words *Our 1st Christmas*. "I've never seen these before. I used to help Mrs. Barton decorate for Christmas, but we never used these gorgeous items."

Eric pulled out a framed, sepia-toned wedding photograph. "Is this your Mrs. B?"

"Yes. She was so beautiful." Jenny wiped a tear from the corner of her eye. "She must've hidden these things away after she lost him. How sad, and so beautifully romantic."

"Romantic?" He eyed her sideways and stood to stretch. And get a bit of much-needed space from the woman he wanted a little more every day.

"Sad and romantic can go together."

The tenderness in her expression sent a surge of longing to his core. As much as he pushed back against her holiday cheer, she kept smiling. Except for when he really got under her skin with his grinchyness. And then she made the cutest expressions that made him want to push back even more.

"You know, Lilly is at the perfect age to start understanding traditions and making those special memories that last forever."

"Sounds like you have lots of good ones. The only good ones I remember were once I was a teen and living with Travis and Martha."

"Want to tell me about some of your memories?"

"No, thanks." He didn't feel like digging too much into his past and messing with his good mood.

"It's never too late to make great memories." Jenny reached into the trunk and lifted out an item wrapped with cloth. It was the model of a house carved out of wood. "Do you know what this is?"

He moved closer and squinted at the little white house. "It's a model of this house." A plaque across the bottom read Happy 10th Anniversary, Forever Yours, William.

"Told you." She sighed and cradled it against her chest. "Romantic."

Girls and their romantic ideas had always baffled him. But somehow, this made sense. *What's gotten into me?*

"I guess she couldn't bear to see these decorations and tucked them away. I'm so glad she hid them. Otherwise, they would've ended up in the estate sale. You bought the house, so they're yours now."

"You can have all of it. It obviously means a lot to you."

"Really? Thank you so much."

She sprang to her feet and wrapped her arms around his waist with such enthusiasm that he swayed and clutched her hips. Heat engulfed him. Instead of using his grip to move her away, he brought them closer together. Body to body. Her cheek resting against his chest. He buried his face in her hair, breathing in her scent. Intoxicating and rapidly stealing his control. And he wished he could kiss her until they were both exhausted.

Why can't I?

Before he had time to talk himself out of it, he let his lips brush her forehead and loved the way her arms tightened around him. When she tipped up her head and her lips parted on a soft sigh, it snapped what little control he had left. Cradling her head, he lowered his mouth to a breath above hers.

Her warm breath feathered over his lips right before she lifted onto her toes, closing the distance between them, sending a hot bolt of desire straight through him. Their soft exploration quickly became deep and heated with a passion he'd never experienced before. So powerful that his whole body felt like a live wire. Her lips were as soft as he'd dreamed, and she tasted like the candy cane she'd been eating.

But this was no dream. She was real and perfect under his hands and mouth.

The jingling of Brad's collar and the sound of Lilly's go-go wheels in the hallway were alarm bells.

Jenny stepped from their embrace, looking as stunned as he felt, and in a rare state of speechlessness. Her flushed cheeks and dazed stare almost made him laugh, but at the same time made him want to pull her back in for more. And see if he could get her to sigh so sweetly again. Surprisingly, he didn't have the urge to flee.

Am I just stunned...or falling for her?

Lilly came through the archway with her usual happy smile. "Daddy, is it Christmas?"

Eric had to clear his throat before he could speak. "Not yet, Lilly Bug. But tomorrow is Thanksgiving." He crossed the room and swooped her into his arms, lifting her way up high until she giggled and held out her arms.

"Lilly, fly over here and see what your daddy found. More Christmas decorations."

"More sparkly?" Lilly asked as he put her down beside her nanny.

"Maybe. Let's see what other treasures are in here." Jenny pulled out a glass angel with golden wings.

"A fairy." Lilly whispered in awe. "Pretty."

"It sure is," Jenny said. "We can add it to the tree."

Eric was still too dazed by their kiss to do much talking right now. And he was happy.

Together the girls lifted a strand of colorful glass mini ornaments that even he recognized as antique.

"More pretty," Lilly said.

In the very bottom of the trunk, they found a

wooden box that contained a set of ten hand-painted ornaments, each with their own specially shaped, satin-lined place. But one of them was missing.

"Where this one?" Lilly asked and poked the empty spot.

"I don't know, sweet girl. But these are amazing." He sat on the couch behind them. "Are they wooden?"

"I think so." Jenny lifted one and handed it to him. "Do you think you can carve a replacement for the missing ornament?"

"I can try, but how will I know what to carve?"

"I bet I can research this set and find out. And if I can't find information, I bet Tess can." She pointed to the lid of the ornaments' box where a gold paper label was peeling up at the corners. "This says Dumbarton, Scotland. McKnight is Scottish, isn't it?"

"Yes. You might find this weird, but when Anson told me the family who built this house was from Scotland, it was the final sign that I should buy it and move here."

Her smile was brighter than the lights on the tree. "I'm glad your last name is McKnight."

"Me, too." He peered more closely into the box. "See all of the Celtic knotwork?"

"Like your tattoo." Jenny bit her lip to hide a grin.

"Which one?" he asked and chuckled at her curious expression.

"How many do you have? I only saw…one."

Her words took him back to being shirtless in

front of her. Touching him with her soft hands. Making him ache with her closeness. "I'll never tell. That's something you'll have to figure out for yourself."

"Have I told you that I can't resist a challenge? Now I'll be on a mission to discover the truth."

That was an idea he could get behind.

Chapter Twelve

Jenny grinned as she wrapped foil around the freshly baked platter of Lilly's Squishies. This batch had extra squishies and looked like mini volcanos of gooey deliciousness with the marshmallow toasted to perfection. Eric walked into the kitchen, and a quick shiver zipped up her spine. The man knew how to wear a sweater and make it look like an advertisement for Highland wool or some manly product. *Stop staring.* "Ready to head over to the town square?"

He leaned against the counter and crossed one booted foot over the other. "Will there be people there?"

"Yes," she said slowly.

"Then, no, thanks."

"Eric, are you really that much of a..." How could she put this without calling him antisocial?

"I think the word you're searching for is *introvert.*"

"I was thinking more along the lines of *recluse.*"

"I guess that works, too." He crossed his arms over his chest. "Have fun tonight."

She gasped. "Are you really not going? There won't be *that* many people."

He rubbed his freshly shaven cheek and grinned. "I'm going. I'd never disappoint my daughter like that. But I have learned to embrace the solitude of my property. Moving out of the city has made me realize I'm an introvert, and this is the escape I've been craving."

Jenny moved a step closer to him. "What were you escaping?"

"The constant motion. And noise."

"You've come to the right place. Oak Hollow moves at a much slower pace. So, no more big cities for you?"

"Nope. I'm done with city life." He pushed away from the counter. "I just need to put Lilly's boots on and we'll be ready."

That figures. Just when a man I'm interested in moves to my small town, I'm moving away to the biggest city in the country.

They were early enough to get a good parking spot along one side of the town square. As they got out of his truck, the sun was making its final descent behind the horizon and putting on a beautiful display. Almost as beautiful as the Christmas lights that would soon be lit.

"Let's button your coat, sweet girl."

Lilly brushed her hand over Jenny's hair as she so often did. "Where we going?"

"To see some Christmas trees and lights and eat some goodies." She put Lilly in her stroller then grabbed the plate of cookies. “Eric, do you have an ice-cream freezer?”

“Other than the one above my refrigerator?” He clipped a leash on Brad and pushed the stroller as they started across the street to the Acorn Café.

“Not that kind. A homemade ice-cream maker. You know, with the crank.” She held the cookies with one hand and imitated turning the handle.

He chuckled. “Nope. Don’t have one of those. And don’t they make the ones that plug into the wall now?”

“Yes, but it’s not as much fun,” Jenny said. “I need to run over to my house for a few other things and I can borrow Mimi’s ice-cream maker.”

“What kind of ice cream are you making?”

“My favorite flavor this time of year is candied Christmas cranberry, but for you I’ll make plain old vanilla.” His fake scowl made her smile. “What? Not a vanilla guy?”

“Sometimes,” he said and then licked his lower lip like he had a wicked idea. “But occasionally I like to taste something new.”

A bolt of desire shot to her very core, and her lips tingled with the desire to kiss him right there in public, but she settled for the sexy smile he gave her. “Good to know.”

The Christmas tree in front of the Acorn Café was real and covered with salt-dough versions of baked goods and twinkling white lights. It was also more crowded than usual, and she hoped Eric wouldn't get twitchy.

"How about you two stay out here with Brad while I run these cookies inside?"

"Good idea," he said and pulled the stroller out of the way.

Jenny squeezed through the crowd in the café and put their entry on the tables set up along the back wall. Mimi had already delivered their cookies, and she looked around for her grandmother. She spotted her sitting at a corner table with Joseph Bailey. The two of them smiled at one another like teenagers. Seeing Mimi like this made Jenny very happy, and she decided not to interrupt them. After filling out a card with Eric's and Lilly's names, she grabbed a couple of candy canes and went outside.

She handed a candy cane to Eric and then Lilly. "Ready to walk around the square and look at all of the Christmas tree entries?"

"Ready-y-y go." Lilly pointed ahead of them and then waved to everyone they passed, and they all smiled and returned her greeting.

But several people studied her and Eric with a bit too much curiosity and a few whispers behind hands. She ignored it but wondered if Eric noticed.

They walked along the rows of businesses that lined all four sides of the quaint town square. The air was cool and filled with the scents of evergreen and hot chocolate from the booth set up on the corner. "I need a cup. Anyone else want any?"

"No, thanks," Eric said around the candy cane sticking out of the corner of his mouth.

"One, please," she said to the young man behind the table. Jenny sipped it to test the temperature, gave Lilly a drink and then wiped whipped cream from the little girl's nose. She could feel Eric watching her and was dying to know what he was thinking behind those moody blue eyes.

The tree in front of the florist shop was flocked and covered with fresh flowers in shades of red and sprigs of holly. Farther down, there was a traditional tree, one made of books displayed at Sip & Read, and one covered with bits of sea glass that shimmered in the lights. Brad sniffed the air as they passed the butcher shop. Their tree was hanging upside down from a meat hook and thankfully not decorated with edible ornaments.

She caught Eric smiling as he watched his daughter's reactions. It was nice to see him enjoying the evening. And she wondered if he was as anxious as she was to share another kiss.

Eric would not admit it, but this small-town celebration wasn't so bad. And watching his little girl's eyes light up at all the decorations was worth every bit of discomfort.

"Look." Jenny pointed across the square. "I see Cody and Luke Walker. Have you met them?"

"I've met Luke." He liked the other man. And if Anson said he was a good guy then he believed it.

"Let's go say hello and see where Alexandra is. Cody is actually Luke's nephew, but they are in the process of adopting him. Cody is on the autism spectrum, so he might not talk to you or want to be touched."

"Got it." He followed Jenny to the other side of the square and had to admit that this little town knew how to do Christmas right. The atmosphere almost took a person back in time.

"Hey, you two," she said.

Eric shook the other man's hand and smiled at the little boy. "Good to see you again."

"You, too." Luke put his arm around Cody's shoulder when the child pressed against him.

"Where's Alexandra?" Jenny asked.

Luke hitched a thumb over his shoulder at Emma's Vintage and shook his head with a grin. "In there. She saw something in the window she just had to have before someone else bought it."

Eric had been shopping with Jenny, and he'd bet the women could keep up with one another.

"Mama Alex shops a lot," Cody whispered, making them chuckle.

Jenny kneeled to his level. "I would like you to meet Lilly. She's new in town."

"Hi." Lilly offered him her half-eaten candy cane.

Cody didn't speak, but he pulled a candy out of his back pocket to show her he had one of his own, but most of his attention was on the dog.

Luke patted his nephew's back. "If you ask, I bet he'll let you pet his dog."

Cody briefly cut his eyes up to Eric and shuffled one boot on the sidewalk.

"You can pet him," Eric said. "His name is Brad and he's very nice."

The little boy held out a hand then smiled when the dog licked him.

Alexandra came out of the store with a shopping bag. A woman with blond hair stepped out behind her.

"Hi, I'm Emma Blake," she said and shook Eric's hand.

"It's nice to meet you." He glanced up at the name of the store. Emma's Vintage. "I guess this is your place?"

"My grandmother's, but she named it after me. It's almost time for them to announce the winners of the cookie contest. We should head over to the gazebo."

Their whole group made their way to the center of the square where everyone gathered. Eric turned his upper body to fit through the crowd without bumping into anyone. Her idea of not many people was still a few too many for him. His short time at Barton Estate had taught him that solitude was a fabulous thing, and he wanted a lot more of it. He could think more clearly—except when Jenny was around. Then he turned into a teenager, or at least his sex drive did.

After Lilly's Squishies won a ribbon for Most Unique, they said their goodbyes and headed for the truck. He stopped in front of a welded metal tree with colored bottles on each branch and examined the way it was built.

"I can see the wheels turning in your brain," Jenny said. "You're thinking about making a Christmas tree out of wood."

He should've been surprised that she knew what he was thinking, but he wasn't. And he liked it. "Maybe so."

"Hey, if you make a wooden tree and some ornaments, I could sew some, and Lilly could..." Her words trailed off as she looked away from him and pressed the tips of her fingers against her mouth.

Eric assessed what she'd said, plus her reaction to her own words. She was talking like they were a family. A family who would be together to do a large project like this next year. He'd lay his money on a bet that Jenny Winslet was fighting a similar internal battle. Both of them asking themselves whether they should resist what felt natural...or dive in and take a chance. "I thought only businesses entered the tree contest?"

"That's true. Never mind." She waved a hand like she was shooing something away. "Let's cross the street at the corner."

Her happy mood had dimmed, and he was even more convinced that they were on the same page of the how-to-start-a-relationship manual. He was good at casual, uncomplicated dating, but he had a feeling Jenny wasn't into that. Still, he'd been wrong before.

* * *

Once they were home and Lilly was in bed, Eric debated his next move. The most sensible thing would be to get in bed and go to sleep. But he wasn't always sensible.

Jenny was a few steps up the staircase when he called her name, unsure what he wanted to happen next but knowing he wanted to see her one more time before he went to sleep. She stopped and slowly turned with her lower lip caught between her teeth. Standing two steps below her put them at eye level, and she was the most desirable woman he had ever met.

"Do you need me?" Her voice was slightly breathless.

Do I need her? That was a loaded question with lots of possible answers. He wanted to carry her to his bed and show her what they both needed. Her mouth on his. His hands on her body.

For her to stay in Oak Hollow.

That last thought kept his feet rooted in place, and his heart hammered against his rib cage. "I just wanted to say thank you for all you're doing for Lilly. And me."

"I'm happy to do all of it."

Her hands flexed at her sides. Did she want to touch him as badly as he wanted it? When she swayed forward, he cupped her cheek and kissed her gently, but before his control snapped completely, he stepped backward down the stairs. "Sleep well, Fairy Woman."

Chapter Thirteen

Thanksgiving Day arrived cold and clear with a slight but unlikely chance of snow. There were so many people at Nan Curry's house that they had to park three houses down from her three-story Victorian. While Eric got Lilly out of her booster seat, Jenny tied a turkey print bandanna around Brad's neck. "There you go, good boy. You're all dressed for the day."

The happy animal rested his head on her shoulder as she hugged him and then he jumped down from the truck.

Jenny grabbed the bag of wine and snack food. "I hope we're in time for me to help with some of the cooking."

"Hope they don't expect me to help cook," Eric said.

"I'll make sure they bar you from the kitchen." She almost took his hand as they met on the sidewalk but managed to restrain herself. Their kiss on the stairway didn't mean they were a couple.

As she introduced Eric to the extended members of the Curry family and the other people he hadn't met, she watched for signs that he would bolt, but he smiled and appeared only mildly uncomfortable. Lilly and Hannah hugged, then took Brad and went to find Cody, who was in the formal living room playing the piano, away from the noise and lively activity of the large group. There was plenty of laughing, eating and catching up with people she hadn't seen in a while.

After the big meal, Tess pulled Alexandra and Jenny out to the sunroom along with a bottle of wine. "Alright, time to tell us what has developed between you and Eric. And don't even try to tell us it's nothing."

"Yes," Alexandra said. "Tell us all the juicy details."

Jenny chuckled. "I see we aren't starting with small talk." She accepted a glass of wine and glanced around to make sure no one else was nearby. "There might have been a few kisses." Her friends clinked their wineglasses as if taking credit for the romantic development. "I'm letting him dictate the pace. But I also recognize anything between us is most likely a bad idea. It will end. The question is how it ends."

"Remember when I came to town with the plan to only stay a month?" Alexandra asked.

"Yes. But Luke didn't have reinforced concrete walls around his heart like Eric does. He has reasons, but I'm not sure he will ever fully open his heart. And he mentioned that he'll never marry again."

"I had some sturdy walls up around myself," Tess said. "They can be busted through. Trust me."

Alexandra laughed and flipped her long red hair over her shoulder. "You guys sound like construction workers with all the talk about concrete and busting through walls. But I think the way you're going about it is right, Jenny. If you sense that he needs it, letting him tell you when he's ready is a smart choice."

"Anson didn't give up on me and now we're a family." Tess topped off each of their glasses. "Do you still want to go away to school?"

Jenny blew out a long slow breath. "I haven't said these words aloud, but I'm starting to second-guess my plan. But altering a plan that's been in place for so many years is a big decision."

"Which way is your pro-versus-con list leaning?" Alexandra asked.

"I don't have one."

"What?" Tess sat forward in her rocking chair. "But you love lists."

Jenny chuckled. Eric had discovered what one of her lists could entail. "I'll start one tonight."

"Good," they both said.

Alexandra held up her pointer finger, not surprisingly stained with several colors of artist's paint. "I have a brilliant idea. I'm taking a quick trip for a wedding in Manhattan between Christmas and New Year's. You should go with me. Maybe checking everything out in person will help you make a decision."

"That's a great idea," Tess agreed.

Cody peeked around the door frame, then stepped into the room. "Mama Alex, time to make whipped cream for pie."

"Okay, we're coming, sweet boy."

They took their glasses and followed Cody to join the rest of the party.

"We're not done discussing your life plan," Alexandra said. "But make your list first."

Jenny recognized how lucky she was to have so many people looking out for her, and her heart was full. But not so full that she didn't have room for a partner to share her love and life with. Could Eric McKnight be the one? Would he ever reconsider his thoughts on marriage?

"The woman is sexy without even trying," Eric said in a hushed tone. There were about twenty other people that didn't need to hear this.

Anson grinned. "You've got it bad, bro." He set his beer on the front porch railing and sat in a wicker chair across from Eric. "I can't say I've ever thought of Jenny that way."

"Dude, how is that possible? I need whatever blinders you're wearing."

"We grew up together, and she's younger. When you are kids, eight years is a big gap. To me she was just a little girl with long braids." He grinned and took a sip of beer. "But she got me good one time. I used to do yard work at Barton Estate, and one day she swung down out of a tree and startled me so bad that I fell backward into the wheelbarrow and rolled down the hill. She came running after me, laughing the whole way."

Eric chuckled at the image in his mind. "That sounds like something my—she would do." *I can't think of her as mine.* "Maybe if I'd seen her as a scrawny kid it would be different." He caught sight of her through the window, laughing with Tess and Alexandra. And his blood surged. Who was he kidding? He couldn't imagine a world where he wasn't attracted to her. And not just the outward beauty that had first caught his eye. There was so much more to her than looks. She radiated something you couldn't see, something mysterious that drew him in a little more each day.

"But I know exactly what you mean about undeniable attraction," Anson said. "When I met Tess, I thought she was the most amazing woman, beautiful even when she was scowling at me. And she did that a lot at first. Kind of like you do."

He jerked his head toward his buddy. "I do what?"

"That blank stare when you don't want anyone to know what you're thinking. I've seen you do it to Jenny."

"Maybe I did. At first." A cold gust of wind sent leaves skittering across the porch and he zipped up his brown leather coat.

"I know it's a defense to hide your feelings. And attraction."

"Wait a minute," Eric said and held up a hand. "Attraction yes. But don't be talking about feelings."

"Come on, McKnight. I see the way you both look at one another when you think the other isn't watching. It's not like you to be indecisive. If you like her and she likes you, what's holding you back?"

"She's moving across the country," Eric said and felt the weight of the words on his heart. *Unless she gets a job at that place in Dallas. It's not so far away.* It wasn't ideal, but it was better than a plane trip. But he could not let himself lay his heart on the line for that slim possibility.

"If she weren't leaving, would you consider a real relationship?"

"I don't have time for fictional delusions. She *is* leaving."

"Not forever. She'll be back. Talk to her about it," Anson said. "I can't imagine her staying there indefinitely. She's a small-town girl whether she realizes it yet or not. And I mean that in a good way. She'll be back. You don't have to tell me but be honest with yourself about your feelings for her."

The front door opened, and Tess, Hannah, Jenny and Lilly stepped onto the porch, saving him not only from answering Anson's question, but from seriously considering it. Lilly was on Jenny's hip, her blond curls almost glowing in the porch light against Jenny's dark hair. They didn't look a thing alike, but they were the two most beautiful creatures he'd ever laid eyes on.

Who was he kidding about feelings not being involved? He'd already considered what it would be like if Jenny were staying in Oak Hollow. And it painted a fairy-tale picture of a dream he shouldn't entertain. She wasn't staying. Period. The end. And he didn't need another goodbye that felt like abandonment or rejection.

He would prepare himself and be ready for the day she left.

"Daddy," Hannah yelled and ran across the porch to hop onto Anson's lap. "Pie time. And cookie, too."

"Thank goodness," Anson said. "I thought I was going to cry I was so hungry."

Hannah clasped his cheeks. "Daddy, you not cry."

"No. I won't cry, little one. Let's go get some before Uncle Luke and Cody eat everything."

Everyone headed for the front door, but Eric remained in the wicker chair.

Jenny paused and looked back at him. *Are you okay?* she mouthed.

"I'm good." Eric stood and followed, rubbing his chest, tight with something that felt a bit too close to...a feeling he didn't want to name. Sharing the duties of taking care of his daughter. Living in the same house. And kisses that rocked his world. There was no stopping this.

Lilly leaned in Jenny's arms and he took her, lingering to inhale their combined scents. "How's my baby girl? Sleepy?"

"Not sleepy, Daddy." But her yawn told a different story.

He met Jenny's smiling eyes and liked that her hand was still resting on his arm. "I think she's had fun with the other kids."

"Definitely," she said. "What do you say we eat dessert then go home?"

He liked the way that sounded coming out of her sweet mouth. "Good idea." He was ready to take her home.

Eric locked his front door and admired the sway of Jenny's hips as she walked in front of him, the top of Lilly's curls visible over one shoulder. He never got tired of seeing them together. Without waking his baby girl, they got her undressed and tucked into bed.

Jenny took his hand and led him from the room. "Did you have fun tonight?"

"I did." And he meant it. "I can see why you talk so fondly about this town." Eric brushed her hair back from her shoulder, and she stopped under the archway to the living room.

"We could build a fire and sit for a while. Wind down from the day before going to bed."

His pulse raced. *Does she mean going to bed alone or together?* "That's a great idea." Eric couldn't deny her request even if he wanted to try. This woman was… Something he couldn't explain. Mysterious. One of a kind.

Before he could start on building a fire, he needed

to kiss her like he'd wanted to do the entire time they were at Anson's. He wrapped her in his arms, and the way she slid her fingers up the back of his neck and into his hair set off a full-body shiver.

It was going to take a team of RECON marines to drag him away from this beautiful woman. Or her giving him any sign that this wasn't what she wanted. When their lips met, her response was instant and filled with the promise of passion. Sweeping his tongue against hers, he loved the way she trembled under his hands.

She moaned and started tugging his shirt from his jeans. "Eric," she whispered.

It was a plea, and his mission was to discover what gave her pleasure. Needing to explore more of her, he kissed his way along her neck, and she arched into him when he nuzzled the spot behind her ear. He wanted her naked and under him. Now.

He lifted his head and cupped her cheek. "Jenny, are you okay with this?" *Please say yes.*

"Yes. I want..." She bit her lip and ducked her head.

With a finger under her chin, he tilted her head to meet his gaze. "Don't get shy on me now. That's not you. Tell me what you want. What you need."

"You." She lifted onto her toes and kissed him so deeply that he swayed.

And that was all the confirmation he needed. Without taking his mouth from hers, he lifted her until her legs wrapped around his waist and he had no idea how he was still standing. Just as he turned to carry her upstairs, the clicking of Brad's nails reached them right before the dog trotted into the room and sat beside them.

Eric inhaled deeply and rested his forehead against hers. "He's telling me that Lilly needs me. I better..."

"Of course. Go. She needs you." She unwound her legs and smoothed down the front of his shirt. "I'll, um... I'm going to go take a shower."

He kissed her once more before following the dog. Apparently, the marines weren't needed to pull him away. All it took was one tiny girl with a riot of curls and the smile of an angel.

Lilly was wiggling and whimpering when he sat on her bedside and stroked her head. "Daddy's here, baby girl."

Her eyes fluttered open, and she reached up to be held. "Daddy, my tummy hurts."

He knew he should've stopped her from eating so many cookies. There would be no going upstairs tonight. Once she was cradled in his arms, he stood and began to sway and sing her favorite lullaby. For the first time since he was young—and tormented by the other boys for singing in the choir—he didn't mind if someone other than his daughter heard him singing.

Chapter Fourteen

When Anson asked Eric to go shopping on the Friday after Thanksgiving, he'd told him he was nuts, but Anson had assured him that shopping in Oak Hollow wasn't the sort of thing you saw on the news. Thankfully, he hadn't lied. Walking along the town square sidewalks there was no crowd to fight, only happy people and no long lines.

"I need to stop in here and buy a pair of pajamas for Hannah," Anson said and pushed through the door of a clothing store. It took a few minutes for them to find the right section but when they did there was an overwhelming selection. "Tess said to get the ones with puppies on them."

"These?" Eric held up a yellow pair with dogs and flowers.

"That must be them. Look, they have matching ones for grownups. I should get a pair for Tess."

While Anson looked for the correct sizes, Eric found a pink pair with dancing fairies. "These are perfect for Lilly." He tucked them under his arm and glanced at the rack of adult sizes.

Anson tossed a pair his way. "This size should work for Jenny."

He took them but didn't respond to his friend's goofball grin.

"Since you've already admitted how you feel about Jenny—"

"Whoa," Eric said. "I didn't admit anything."

"Whatever you say. I just hope you let yourself enjoy your time with her while she's here," Anson said and headed for a jewelry display.

He'd sure enjoyed kissing her last night, but he didn't need to admit that and give Anson more ammunition. "I knew moving here meant you'd get me into some kind of trouble. I just didn't expect it to be in the form of a woman."

Anson barked a laugh. "Don't blame this on me. Unless it works out really well. Then I'll take credit." With a pair of earrings selected, he headed for the register.

Back out on the sidewalk, they made their way to the other side of the square to buy toys at Mackintosh's Five & Dime.

"How are the plans coming for your restoration business?" Anson asked.

"I haven't done much yet. After Chris Lopez and his guys start working on my house, I'll see if they have the skill and work ethic I'm looking for. I'm not rushing anything."

"I was just talking to the city council about the revitalization going on in the area. People wanting to get out of the city and such. We need someone like you in the area."

"That's good to hear. When I first got to Oak Hollow, I was worried I'd have to eventually move to a big city again, but this area of the Hill Country has so many historic homes. While driving around, I've noticed many that need repair. But what was I thinking buying such a big house for two of us?"

"You could get married and have more kids to fill up some of the rooms."

"You really want me settled down as much as you, don't you?"

"I just want to see you happy."

They passed a group of young women who smiled with a round of cheery hellos and started giggling after they'd gone by.

Eric glanced over his shoulder and one of them waved and fluttered her lashes. "Is that normal?" he asked his friend.

"The word has gotten around that you're single. Should I tell everyone you're off the market?"

Eric didn't answer, because he wanted to say yes.

Jenny parked in front of Queen's Sew 'n' Sew then hopped out and opened the back door. "Ready to shop, sweet girl?"

"Ready." Lilly held up her arms to be unbuckled from her booster.

The delight on her cherub face made Jenny want to gather her up for a hug and smell the lavender scent of her baby shampoo. And that's exactly what she did. Her heart had fallen hard for this sweet, motherless child.

Lilly kissed her cheek. "More Christmas?"

"Yes. We're going to buy Christmas fabric. Want to walk or me to carry you?"

"You do it." Lilly giggled as she tried to catch fall leaves dancing in the wind.

"Can you help me pick out cute fabric to make dresses for you and your new friend Hannah?"

"For me?"

"Yes, for you. And there's a whole room with fabric just for kids."

Every person in the shop rushed over to meet one of the town's newest residents. They oohed and aahed over her blond curls and happy personality.

"The word is that this little one's father is very easy on the eyes," said one of the shoppers.

Jenny prayed she wouldn't blush. "He's nice-looking." She'd leave out her belief that he was worthy of being named sexiest man alive.

"And—" the other woman leaned in close to whisper "—the word around town is that you're *living* with him."

A weight plummeted into Jenny's stomach. *Oh no! This is not good.*

They got home before Eric and had just finished mixing up the ice cream when he came through the back door. His arms were loaded with shopping bags, and his smile led Jenny to believe that he had not heard the rumor about them while shopping with Anson.

"Hello, ladies."

"Look, Daddy," Lilly said from her booster seat at the table. "We make ice cream."

"Yum. What flavor? Broccoli?"

"No." Lilly stuck out her tongue. "That's yucky."

He set his bags on the floor and kissed the top of his daughter's head, and Jenny wished he would give her a hello kiss, too. It might be the last chance if he got upset when she told him about the rumor going around.

"Are we having ice cream for dinner?" he asked.

"We're having a roast chicken meal that we picked up at the Acorn Café." She crossed to them with a wet towel for Lilly's sticky hands. "We can eat as soon as we get the ice cream churning."

"Are you going to make me crank the handle to earn my dinner?"

She chuckled then caught his scent of leather and wood and swayed toward him. "I was just teasing you about that. Lucky for you, this one plugs in. You're off the hook."

"In that case, I think you two ladies need an early Christmas present." He handed each of them a gift bag and Lilly immediately tossed the red and green tissue and laughed when Brad snatched it out of the air. She pulled out a pair of pink flannel pajamas.

“Oh my gosh, those are so adorable,” Jenny said. “Look what’s on them.”

“Fairies!” The little girl hugged them to her chest.

“Open yours,” Eric said with a shy smile.

Her bag contained a matching pair, and she couldn’t resist hugging them just like Lilly. “I love them. Thank you so much.”

“You’re welcome. You two can take a picture in your matching pj’s by the tree.”

She gasped. “We didn’t put taking a photo with Santa on the list.”

“How’d you forget that one? They might take away your Mrs. Christmas status,” he teased and gave her a quick kiss. “I’m going to put away the rest of the stuff I bought and then I’ll come back and help.”

“Sounds good.” She rubbed her lips, still tingling from his kiss, and couldn’t resist watching him walk from the room. The man certainly knew how to wear a pair of jeans.

Dinner and ice cream were finished and cleaned up. Lilly’s bath and night-night tuck in time was completed. And she didn’t have any more excuses for putting it off. Jenny took a deep breath and readied herself to tell Eric what she’d learned while in town with Lilly. He was kicked back on the sectional couch with a detective novel, and she stopped halfway into the room. “So, I heard a rumor today while I was at the fabric store.”

"Don't leave me hanging," he said in a deadpan voice and closed the book. "The suspense is too much."

"Buckle up for this one. There's a rumor going around town that we are more than friends and living together in *all* ways." Her pulse beat a rapid rhythm in her throat, but she closed the distance between them. "Are you upset?"

With his elbows on his knees, he studied her for a few beats before answering. "No. And I'm not that surprised. I've seen the way people watch us."

Some of the tension released from her shoulders. This was a good response. So much better than the scenarios she'd worked up in her mind.

"Want to sit?" he asked.

When she hesitated, trying to judge how close to sit, he patted the cushion next to him. But he wore his blank expression. She took the spot he indicated and was tempted to stroke the curve of his face and see if his response would give her a feel for his thoughts.

As if he'd read her mind, he brushed her hair over her shoulder, his fingers trailing across her neck. "I gave up worrying about what other people say a long time ago. I had to if I was going to survive in my world."

She released the breath she'd been holding. "I wish I could master that ability."

His brow furrowed. "Does it bother you that much that people are talking about us?"

"No. I mean it's annoying that people can't mind their own business, but I was more worried you'd be upset."

He held her captive with his blue eyes. "I've been told that our mutual attraction is obvious. And I don't see any point in denying it any longer."

Diva and Pollyanna shared a high-five and hip bump, and Jenny's smile grew wide enough to make her cheeks ache. "Were you denying it because I work for you or because I'm…leaving?" *Or because you won't let anyone into your heart?*

He draped his arm across the back of the couch and stroked her hair. "I guess it's both. But I'm used to people leaving. Everything is temporary. The only thing that's forever is being Lilly's father. That's something I cannot fail at. It's not an option."

His words made her stomach clench and hung a cloud over her good mood. "I don't see any risk of you failing with Lilly. You're an amazing father." But he believed everything else was temporary and it sounded like that included her.

Will he ever trust anyone enough to open his heart again?

Eric studied the beautiful face of the most intriguing woman he'd ever met. So caring. So full of fun. And amazing with Lilly. Could Jenny also be an amazing partner? Because it sure felt natural to put his arm around her.

"Will you tell me something about Lilly's mother?"

His lungs constricted as they always did at the thought of Cilia. "I don't really talk about her."

"I'm sorry. I shouldn't have asked."

When she made to stand up, he tightened his arm around her shoulders. "Stay. Please." He got that knot of guilt in the pit of his stomach. The one that cut deep every time he thought about being the reason Lilly didn't have a mother. They'd already been headed for divorce before she gave birth, but he'd thought they'd still co-parent in the same city. That his child would have two parents.

Jenny leaned her head against his shoulder. "I'll listen if you want to tell me, but you don't have to say another word about it."

Before he could overthink anything, he started talking. "We got married because she was pregnant. Halfway into the pregnancy, she started questioning whether she wanted to be a parent, and I started questioning my decision to marry her." He paused and took a deep breath. "Once Lilly was born but still in the neonatal ICU, Cilia took a job in England without even talking to me about it. And she did not expect us to go with her."

Jenny snuggled closer against his side, showing her support without saying a word.

"I told her she could not take the job and leave her daughter." He stopped and cleared his throat in an effort to hide the turbulent emotions this topic raised. Telling Cilia what to do had been a horrible mistake.

"I can understand why her doing that would trigger bad memories." She smoothed the front of his shirt then left her hand resting over his heart.

Goose bumps rose under her tender touch. Jenny recognized how his wife's actions had set off childhood trauma, but his wife never had. "She said I couldn't tell her what to do. We didn't sleep in the same room, so it was easy for her to leave in the middle of the night. And I never saw her alive again."

And it was my fault.

"How did..."

"Car accident."

"And Lilly was still in the hospital when she left?"

"Yes. She was premature. Weighed four and a half pounds."

"You were alone to deal with a newborn and your business?"

And my gut-wrenching guilt that she died sneaking away from me in the middle of the night. "I had some friends and employees that helped me out when I needed it most."

She wrapped her arm around him, and he kissed the top of her head. He never expected people to stick around forever. They usually left sooner than later. Like Jenny would do before the end of January. And even though he knew it was pointless, he still found himself wishing she would stay in Oak Hollow. But at least he had time and would be prepared for her leaving.

Suddenly, he didn't want to waste any time that he could have with this beautiful woman. "Since everyone already believes we're sharing a bed…what do you say to making it true?" Her wide smile made a fairy-tale future flash before his eyes, and his heart skipped a beat.

What door did I just throw open? Did I just suggest we live as a real couple?

"I'm not saying…" He cleared his throat. "I'm not trying to rush you or…"

She put a finger against his lips. "Let's start slow and see what happens."

Even though he'd just freaked himself out with the proposal, her answer was disappointing, but if she wanted to take it slow, he would. "Good plan."

"I heard you singing to Lilly last night. You really do have an amazing voice. Why don't you use it?"

Since he was already spilling his guts, he might as well get this out of the way, too. "It goes back to the time I lived in a group home. I was about ten and I started singing in the church choir. Some of the other boys made fun of me and even beat me up." The memory still made his skin feel hot and too tight.

Jenny put her hand over his. "That's…" Her voice cracked. "I can't imagine what that must've been like. It breaks my heart that you had to go through something like that."

He shrugged. "Made me stronger. And tougher."

"You don't always have to be tough, at least not around me."

He cupped her cheek and stroked her soft lips with his thumb. At the moment, he couldn't find words, so he kissed her and put all of the things he couldn't say into the kiss, and she responded with an enthusiasm that made his blood surge. They made out on the couch like teenagers, and somehow, they managed to keep their clothes on, but his heart was another story and had been bared to whatever was coming.

Chapter Fifteen

Jenny tried sketching, reading, music, meditation—which had never worked—and nothing was helping her fall asleep. Eric's suggestion to share a bed had taken her by surprise, and she'd been about to wholeheartedly agree but the flash of alarm on his face had stopped her. But now she regretted so quickly saying they should take it slow. They didn't have time for taking it slow.

Why didn't I just take him by the hand and lead him upstairs?

Thinking about him while tossing and turning in bed made her only want to fill the empty space beside her. And all she could think about was the way he'd kissed her good-night at the foot of the stairs, setting her whole body ablaze. His talented mouth on hers. His hands cradling her so tenderly. What would it be like to feel his big gentle hands, skin to skin, on every part of her body? Her pulse fluttered like a hummingbird, and she was more awake than ever.

"This line of thinking certainly isn't helping."

Double-checking that the coffee pot's timer was set correctly was the perfect excuse for a trip to the kitchen, where the rest of the homemade ice cream just happened to be. She slid out of bed and tiptoed down the front staircase, avoiding the two squeaky treads. It was cooler downstairs, and she wished she'd put on the bottoms of her new fairy pajamas, but she'd never been able to sleep in pants.

The coffeepot was ready, just as she'd known it would be. After choosing one of Lilly's small plastic bowls for portion control, she filled it with the soft, creamy deliciousness and set it aside to soften further while she made a cup of hot chocolate. The moon was full and bright, and she leaned on the counter to admire the view. Bare branches danced in the wind, frosted in shimmery light. She took her first bite, sweetness melting on her tongue. "Mmm. You make my mouth so happy."

A sweeping shadow and distinctly male bark of laughter startled her into a spin, and her full spoon of ice cream splattered across Eric's bare chest. Her heart settled back into place. "You scared the pants off me," she said breathlessly once she could speak.

Eric wore a sexy grin as his gaze swept along her bare legs. "You're not wearing pants."

"And you're not wearing a shirt. But you are wearing my ice cream. Sorry."

"No apology necessary."

Jenny dropped the silverware back into the bowl, grabbed a dish towel and rushed forward to wipe his chest. His very bare, muscled, hard chest.

He stood completely still but his breathing accelerated, and his eyes focused on her hand, following every move.

Pausing with the towel pressed against his six-pack, Jenny met his gaze. And he didn't need to speak to tell her what he was thinking. The desire was in the way he held his body, the set of his mouth. The intense longing in his blue eyes as he backed her up against the counter.

"Would you like to share my ice cream?" Her voice was breathless, and she wondered if he could hear the eagerness in her tone.

"Yes, I would," he whispered with his mouth close to her ear. "And I'd also like to see if I can make your mouth as happy as the ice cream."

A delightful shiver pulsed through her and the towel dropped to the floor. Eric grasped her hips and lifted her onto the counter, his eyes holding her in a trance that she was happy to fall into.

After dipping his finger into the bowl, he spread ice cream across her lips, then slowly lowered his mouth to hers, teasing her with his tongue. "Mmm. Delicious. I want more," he said.

Their lips brushed softly for only a moment before he took her in a kiss that proved toe curling was not a myth. Exploring every part of her mouth. Urging her to take everything he offered. Wanting to touch him everywhere at once, she clutched his shoulders, tangled her fingers in his hair and dove into his tender but frenzied attention.

He chuckled when she moaned but inhaled sharply

when she wrapped her legs around him, pressing her heels into his butt and pulling him snuggly against her. There was no hiding how much he wanted her.

She would not be suggesting they take it slow this time. Not when she was wrapped around the man invading her dreams and senses. The grumbly bear who had a heart of gold hidden under his gruff exterior, and who was more mouthwatering than any sweet treat. When his hand slipped under her shirt and slid slowly up her sides, thumbs brushing the sides of her breasts, she moaned and arched into his touch. The scent of his skin making her head swim.

"Taking it slow is overrated," she said breathlessly.

"Agreed. Hold on to me, sweet thing."

His husky voice hummed through her, striking a desire that even the most prim and proper Pollyanna couldn't resist. And when he cupped her bottom in his hands and turned to leave the kitchen, she might have whimpered. "Where are we going?"

"If you don't have any objections, upstairs."

"You won't hear me arguing. But you can't carry me up the whole flight of stairs."

"Watch me."

She tightened her arms around his neck as he climbed the staircase, the shifting of his steps zinging sparks to her very center. "You're not going to fire me if we do this, are you?"

"I was about to beg you not to quit."

They both laughed as he carried her through the door of her room and laid her gently onto the bed. Instead of releasing her hold, she scooted farther onto the mattress and pulled him down with her, his hips nestled between her thighs. Braced on his hands above her, he stared at her with a new expression. One she hadn't seen before, filled with intensity and passion. And she liked it.

His skin was hot and smooth and covering more sculpted muscles than she'd ever had the pleasure of touching. And she wanted to drown in his heartbreak-blue eyes. When he shifted his hips, she was hit with tingles. The kind that make your vision waver.

"Tell me what you need, fairy woman."

"Everything. You. Kiss me again."

"Gladly." Lowering to his forearms, he sucked her lip then nipped it with his teeth before sweeping his tongue skillfully over hers.

With one flick, he released her top button and trailed a line of kisses from her mouth to her shoulder. One more button and his mouth moved lower. Chill bumps erupted in such close proximity that she felt weightless and was convinced she was floating.

A satisfied groan rumbled in his chest a second before he opened the last button.

His touch was filled with all the fireworks and passion she'd only read about. But beyond the physical, there were feelings, deep feelings that made her heart flutter.

* * *

Eric looked into Jenny's soulful eyes and vowed to remember this moment forever. The excitement coursing through him. The eagerness returned in her touch. The desire and promise in her kisses.

"Will Brad be able to find us?" she whispered.

"Yes." He caressed her cheek, loving that she cared enough to think of Lilly. And not because it was her job. It was something more. Pressing his lips to her neck, he inhaled, intoxicated by her taste and scent. All woman with a sweetness he'd never experienced.

Her hands trailing from his shoulders to low on his hips made heat blaze and spread until his entire body was hot enough to melt a glacier. He rolled onto his back, taking her with him to straddle his hips. The movement of her shiver had him ready to burst under her. In slow exploration, he slid his hand along her soft thighs, over the curves of her hips and up farther. When she arched into his touch, her pajama top slipped from her shoulders, her skin glowing in the moonlight streaming through the windows.

"You are so beautiful. So sexy."

"You make me feel alive. And I think it's time to search for more of your tattoos." She lowered until they were skin to skin.

And there went the last of his restraint. They caught fire and lost themselves in one another. Long kisses. Lingering touches. Soft whispers filled with hope and promise.

And he took them both to a place of bliss.

* * *

Hours later, with Jenny's head resting on his chest, he hummed softly and stroked the length of her back.

"Will you sing to me?" She kissed his chest and gazed up through thick lashes.

Out of habit, he started to say no, but realized he wanted to sing. This one of a kind woman made him want to sing. With Jenny wrapped in his arms, he quietly sang "You Are So Beautiful" until she drifted to sleep.

Saturday morning arrived with misty rain and thick cloud cover, but Jenny's mood was anything but dreary. Eric's morning kiss had seen to that, and assured her their night together hadn't catapulted him back into being the distant man she'd first met. The magical experience was one she'd relive over and over and over again.

But right now, it was time to focus and not burn the waffles. She removed one and poured more batter into the waffle iron.

Lilly clanged two metal measuring cups together. "More bacon, please."

"Only one more piece or there won't be any left for your daddy." She gave her half of a strip.

"Yummy." She broke off a small piece and gave it to the dog before Jenny could stop her.

"Did you just feed Brad from the table?"

Lilly held up her hands and tipped her head with her cutest doe-eyed expression. "Hannah said share."

Jenny turned her head so Lilly wouldn't see her smile. "She's right. Sharing is very nice, but your daddy said not to feed Brad from your plate."

The little girl went back to stacking the measuring cups, and the dog signaled he needed to go outside. After opening the kitchen door for him, she pulled the last waffle from the waffle iron then lifted Lilly. "Alright, sweet girl, let's go tell Daddy that breakfast is ready."

"I walk. No go-go."

"Okay. We can do that." Jenny held her hands and noticed that she was bearing more of her own weight today. It made her heart happy that Lilly was moving with more comfort because of something she had designed. But she could make it better. This design needed one adjustment to be almost perfect.

They came around the corner into the living room. Eric was kneeling on the floor cleaning ashes from the hearth, and he was humming a Christmas song. Jenny wanted to freeze the moment like a Norman Rockwell painting. Seeing him relaxed and happy pulled her deeper into his spell, like this really was the Beast's magic castle with dancing furniture.

"Daddy," Lilly squealed.

He shifted to one knee to face them, a huge smile on his face. "Look at you, big girl. Good job." His gaze flicked up to Jenny, and his true smile remained. The one that was so big it made his eyes narrow and his high cheekbones stand out.

Just having his eyes on her sent her heart racing, and she returned his smile to the point that her cheeks ached. He was letting her in a little more each day. Trusting her with his past. But what exactly *did* his attitude mean?

What do I want it to mean?

Lilly took a few more steps and hugged him. "Daddy, ice cream, please."

The words *ice cream* made Eric chuckle, and Jenny felt the warmth of a blush rising. She knew exactly what she wanted his attitude to mean. For him to never regret last night. To continue opening up. To want her in their lives.

"We can have ice cream after we eat breakfast. If Jenny didn't eat all of it," he teased.

Lilly turned to her with an outraged expression that was so cute, she wanted to cover her with kisses. "I promise I did not eat all the ice cream. Breakfast is ready and we should eat before it gets cold."

"Good. For some reason I woke up with an extra big appetite this morning." He winked at Jenny then put Lilly on her feet and took her hands. "Ready to walk to the kitchen?"

"Ready," she said and gave a little hop then wobbled but quickly righted herself.

Slow and steady, with loads of patience and love, he walked his daughter to the kitchen then lifted her into her booster seat. "After we eat, I'll build a fire. It's going to stay cold and wet all day. I'll have to put off the work I'd planned to do on the playhouse."

Jenny put waffles and bacon on the table then

rested her hand on his shoulder. “Are you taking the day off?”

“I guess I am.” He turned his head enough to kiss the top of her hand.

That’s all it took to make her tingle from head to toe. “And tonight, we can watch another Christmas movie?” Jenny asked and took her seat.

While pouring syrup on his waffle, he pretended to be upset by it and pulled a face that made Lilly laugh. “Only if I get to pick the movie.”

“Sure. What would you like to watch?”

“I’ve heard that some people consider *Die Hard* to be a Christmas movie.”

His mischievous grin made Jenny laugh. “Not when you have a child watching. But if you’re a good boy, we can watch it after tuck-in time.”

“We might be too busy doing something else at that time,” he whispered.

Lilly and Brad were playing beside the Christmas tree and knocked a red plastic ball off a low-hanging branch. It rolled across the floor and stopped at Eric’s feet.

“You two be careful. You don’t want to break one.” Eric picked it up, tossed the ornament into the air then caught it. “Ho-ho-ho.”

“I think you’re the one who needs to be careful.” Jenny said. “Your holiday cheer is showing.”

“Bah humbug.” One of his eyebrows went up in a villainous expression.

"And here I thought I was helping you see the magic."

With an arm around her waist, he nestled her against his side. "You're working miracles on this Scrooge." He nuzzled her ear and whispered, "And you helped me see the magic. Last night. In your bed."

Chill bumps raced across her skin and she wrapped both arms around his waist. "I'm happy to be your magician, anytime."

Chapter Sixteen

On Sunday, the rainy weather had ended, and the bright sunshine was drying everything out. A light breeze carried the scent of damp leaves. Jenny buttoned Lilly's sweater and opened her package of animal crackers. "Stay here on the blanket with Brad while your daddy and I finish working."

"And clean my playhouse?"

"That's right." She turned to watch Eric cut a small sapling that was brushing against the outer wall. "I'm so happy the inside is in such good condition."

"It was made well. But I'll have to replace some exterior wood and repaint everything."

She swept leaves and dirt from the stepping-stones in front of the door. "I love this little house."

Eric yanked a trailing vine off the playhouse with what looked like more force than necessary, then spun to face her. "Why are you so eager to leave Oak Hollow? You're always telling me how much you love this or that."

Surprised by the abruptness of his question, Jenny opened her mouth to repeat one of the standard answers. To see more of the world. To do what she loved. To have a career. But not for the first time, doubt about her plans held her tongue.

The list her girlfriends had encouraged her to start had ten reasons to stay in Oak Hollow. While the reasons to go to school column had only three. *It's the plan. Career opportunities. Adventure.*

Still clutching a handful of vines, he stood there with what looked like sadness in his eyes and waited for her to respond.

"It's been my dream for a long time." *But dreams can change.* Even though he'd told her he was used to people leaving and expected it, she suspected it was harder on him than he'd admit.

He tossed the vines onto the brush pile. "I'm sorry. I shouldn't have said that." They worked in silence for a few minutes before he turned to her with an understanding but sad smile. "How long will you be in school?"

"At first, I wanted to pursue a four-year bachelor's, but because I'm already twenty-seven, the two-year associate's is a better option."

"And you'll stay in New York after you graduate?"

"No." She propped the broom against a tree. "When I was young, I wanted to stay and live in the city and work in a big fashion house, but it's too far away from everyone I love. I'll come back to Texas."

"To Oak Hollow?"

Is he asking because he wants me to come home? To him? Her heartbeat sped, and she had to lean against the playhouse. "Possibly. Or one of the larger cities nearby. Loren Lane isn't the only one in the area."

"Are you still going to send them some of your stuff?"

"Yes. But I have to get the designs perfect before sending them." Could this opportunity turn into an acceptable reason to forgo school? She rubbed her temples, hoping to hold off a tension headache this life-altering decision sometimes caused. More and more she was considering changing her plans, but she could not say anything to Eric until she knew with 100 percent certainty what she'd do. Right then and there she decided two things. She would wait to make her final decision until after she went to New York with Alexandra and after she heard from Loren Lane.

Lilly tossed a tennis ball for the dog and clapped when he spun in a circle before racing across the yard. "Go, Brad."

She smiled at Lilly then turned her attention to Eric, who was watching her the same way she did his child. She wanted to believe the expression on his face was growing affection, but there was turmoil in his eyes. And she hoped he didn't start retreating from their new closeness.

He wiped his hands on his jeans then pulled her into a hug. With her head resting on his chest, the steady beat of his heart soothed her.

"Do you want to paint this playhouse white again?" he asked.

"I think so. That way it matches the big house." She was glad for the change of subject before she made a rash decision and said she'd stay with them forever. But Eric hadn't asked her to stay forever. She swallowed the knot that appeared in her throat. Why was she being so indecisive about her future?

It was just fear of the unknown. Being nervous about a major life change. Not because she had fallen in love with this man and his adorable child.

But that's exactly what she had done. She'd fallen in love.

At Lilly's request, they both did her night-night tuck-in time together. After one story from a book, Jenny told another adventure of the fairy that lived under the red toadstool. Lilly was finally sleeping peacefully, her blond curls framing her cherub face.

When Eric took Jenny's hand, led her into his bedroom and closed the door, tingles shimmered across her skin. "You're allowing me into your bedroom?" She slid a hand under the front of his T-shirt and smiled when he shivered.

"Only if you want to be here." He tipped up her chin.

"I do."

"Good. My bed is bigger."

His bed was also covered with books he'd sorted into three piles. "It looks like we need to finish putting those away first."

Pulling her closer, he kissed his way up her neck. "We could just rake them onto the floor."

She giggled and rubbed her hands along the muscles of his arms. "You can't treat your book collection like that. It will only take a few minutes with the two of us."

He growled and pulled a face. "Fine. Let's get it done. The biographies go on the bottom shelf. Start with those, and I'll put the mystery novels on top."

They moved the stacks to the floor in front of the shelves. As she lowered to sit, she let her hand slide along the polished dark wood of the ornate trim work. Her index finger slipped into the largest of the decorative grooves. She leaned closer to study the indention. There were staggered layers carved deeper and deeper, and one side was slightly different from the other. Chills erupted and she sucked in a sharp breath.

"Oh my green goddess. I think this pattern is the reverse of one point on the star."

Eric came up close behind her. "It does look that way. Where's the star?"

"On my bedside table upstairs."

"I'll get it." He kissed the top of her head and walked away.

While he was gone, she ran her finger along the length of the molding she could reach. On the right side, she hit a raised spot about the size of the head of a thumb tack. "This must mean something."

"What did you find?" Eric asked as he reclosed the door.

"Come see."

"It's definitely a place to start." He put the star in her hand and smiled. "Try it."

When she fitted it into the grooves right above the odd protrusion, she felt the tug of strong magnets connecting. She gasped and took her hand off the key, and it stayed in place. "I can't believe it. This is it. We found it."

"You found it, fairy woman. Aren't you going to see what happens next?"

"Absolutely. I just wanted to savor the moment." The only direction to go was up, so with a deep breath, she took hold of the star and pushed it up along the groove. It took more pressure than expected. Scraping and shuddering sounds came from inside the wall and it became harder to move the key right before a clunk sounded, like something dropped into place. The whole built-in shifted slightly away from the wall, and little swirls of dust puffed around the border.

With the star clutched in her hand, she did a little happy dance. "I can't believe we found it."

He chuckled and put the star on one of the shelves. "Let's see what's inside."

They grabbed the edge of the bookcase and slowly pulled it open. The creaking whine of rusty hinges made all of her senses tingle. The dark space was only big enough for them to go through one at a time.

"We need a flashlight and shoes." He went to his bedside table and pulled a yellow flashlight from the drawer.

Once they were wearing shoes, they stepped into the narrow space, barely wider than the width of Eric's shoulders. It smelled a bit musty, and dust motes floated in the beam of his flashlight like tiny ghosts. To their left, a spiral staircase led up to a tiny second floor landing and then up farther to the attic. To the right there was a dust-covered stone bench. And in front of them, there was another door with a latch and an assortment of gears.

"The library is on the other side of this wall isn't it?" she asked.

"I believe so. What was it Mrs. Barton told you about the star?"

"It will open secret places in my heart and take me into the past. I guess this was her secret place. Mrs. Barton asked to see me, right before she died, but I didn't make it in time. I bet this is what she wanted to tell me about." The thrilling moment was tinged with a touch of sadness. She really missed the kind woman who'd been like a great-grandmother to her.

Eric stepped behind her and wrapped his arms around her waist. "Probably so. What should we explore first?"

"Let's see if this does in fact lead into the library." Since they were inside the narrow passageway, they were able to lift the latch by hand. They slowly pushed it forward and the dark library came into view.

"Tomorrow we'll have to figure out how to open it from the other side."

"Let's see where the stairs lead." She turned to go up, but he grabbed her hand.

"Wait. Those stairs are old, and I need to check them to see if they're safe. Hold this light for me."

She waited impatiently while he made his inspection.

"I'm going to go up first and make sure they're sturdy," he said.

Her nerves rattled. "What if they aren't safe and you fall?"

"I'm sure you have Dr. Clark on speed dial." He winked at her.

"I have the number memorized. It's been the same since I was a child. Be careful, please."

Eric's size made it a bit of a challenge for him to navigate the spiral staircase and small treads. Once he deemed it safe, he motioned to her. "Start coming up very slowly so I can make sure nothing shifts."

One step at a time, she climbed to his level. On the second floor, a small panel slid to the side and opened into a closet. At the top, a trap door opened into the attic.

Once they were back on the ground floor, Jenny walked over to the small stone bench only big enough for one person to sit. A box of candles and matches sat on top, everything covered with a thick layer of dust.

Eric shone the flashlight under the bench. "There's something under there."

"I'll get it." She lowered to her knees and pulled out a weather-proof lockbox. "Hell yes! I think we've found another treasure."

"I think you're right, but it isn't as old as the trunk from the attic. I know this kind of lockbox, and it's maybe ten years old at the most."

"But what's inside of the box could be old."

"True," he said then brushed a cobweb from her hair and gave her a quick kiss. "Let's take it to the bedroom where there's more light."

Adrenalin had her pulse thrumming as she followed him into the bedroom.

My house has a secret passageway. How cool is that?

Jenny's excitement was contagious, and Eric had to admit he found this discovery exhilarating, and he couldn't wait to study the way it was built. "Let's see if it's locked." After scooting books aside, he set the dusty box on his bedside table, squeezed both sides of the release button and it opened. A stack of letters was tied with a faded pink ribbon and a small black velvet jewelry box rested in one corner.

"This is so much fun," she said and did a little hip shimmy.

The movement was one he hoped she'd repeat in bed. He rubbed his eyes and tried to focus on what they were doing at the moment. "Is this romantic like the trunk full of decorations?"

"Definitely." She picked up the velvet box and pulled back the lid. "Oh. My. Goodness. This is gorgeous."

"Whoa." A diamond ring with a center stone that had to be at least two carats sparkled in the lamplight. "This really is a treasure."

"Maybe it was her engagement ring, but I never saw her wear it." Slipping it from the box, she put it on her finger. "It fits. I wonder if she meant for me to find this?"

While Jenny admired the ring, he opened a large envelope that filled the bottom of the lockbox. Inside of it was a certificate of authenticity for the ring and a letter. And the letter was addressed to Jenny. "She definitely meant for you to find this." He handed it to her and watched her eyes grow wide as she read.

"This ring is worth a lot of money. And she wanted me to have it." She read aloud.

I tucked this away just for you because I want you to make your dreams come true. Never give up on your dreams!

His chest tightened at the thought of her going off to follow her dreams. "She sure took a risk that you would never find it." Jenny sat on the bed and squinted as if looking at something he couldn't see.

"If you hadn't bought this house and hired me as Lilly's nanny, I never would have found it. And what are the chances. But…Mrs. Barton did tell me she had visions of the future."

"Like a fortune teller?"

"I never thought of it that way. I thought she meant something more like daydreams or that it was just something she told me like the make-believe stories about magical creatures." She smiled at him. "I guess she had faith, or she really could see into the future and knew that I would find it. But I don't think I could ever sell it. If that's even what she had in mind."

His house sure held a lot of secrets and mystery. "The letter doesn't say what she wanted you to do with it?"

"No. Mainly just to follow my dreams."

"Maybe there's a clue in one of these other letters." He pulled the top one from the stack. "Look at the postmark."

"It's from her husband when he was overseas. But maybe I shouldn't read her private letters."

"If she put them in this box, I would assume she wanted you to read them."

She clasped the bundle against her chest. "I guess you're right. I'll read one a day to make them last. I bet these will tell me something about her marriage and who knows what else. It will be a look into the past."

A chill raced across his skin. He didn't want a look at *his* past. He wanted to look to the future. One he hoped she'd be a part of. How could he keep her close and not take away her dream?

"Eric, did you hear me? Are you okay?"

"I'm fine. You need to keep that ring somewhere safe."

"I guess putting it back where we found it is the safest place I can think of."

"True."

She wiped dust from her black shirt. "We're all dirty now," she said, and a slow grin lifted the corners of her mouth. "Maybe we need a shower?"

That snapped him right back to the present. "You have some of the best ideas."

Eric was tired from keeping Jenny up late the night before. And the one before that. But it was totally worth it. He put the piece of decorative trim in place, but it still didn't fit properly. He resisted hurling it across the room.

"I need some fresh air." He opened the French doors of the upstairs bedroom and stepped onto the balcony. The afternoon was mild and sunny, and he was thankful there was no snow to shovel, but he was starving and needed a break. The scene below brought a smile to his face. All his frustration melted away.

Jenny, Lilly and Brad were circled around something on the ground under a tree in the front yard. All three of them had their butts in the air as they intently studied something near the base of the biggest oak. With a big smile, he rested his forearms on the railing and watched to see what they would do next.

Brad barked and wagged his tail. Lilly's giggle mixed with Jenny's laugh and his hunger was forgotten. The sound was better than any drug. He still had no idea what they were looking at, but he was as mesmerized by the sight of them as they were by the mystery object. They were probably looking for fairies under mushrooms.

Once they finished their investigation, Jenny held his daughter's hands while they walked around the yard, encouraging her with every step. Then the trio settled on a blanket under the pecan tree. He watched them for so long, Lilly fell asleep with her head on Jenny's leg and Brad curled up beside her. Jenny had her back propped against the tree trunk and was reading a novel. The clouds shifted and the sun hit her dark hair, making it shimmer. Lilly would say it looked like fairy hair.

She put her book aside and stroked Lilly's curls. The sweetness of her smile stole his next breath.

My girls. Eric straightened and rubbed a hand across his chest. This feeling was not supposed to happen. He wasn't supposed to…

Fall in love.

But he had. He'd fallen in love with Jenny Winslet.

Chapter Seventeen

Jenny twirled one of Lilly's baby-soft curls around her finger and glanced up at the sound of crunching leaves. Eric walked across the yard to their afternoon alfresco nap spot, the easy, honest smile on his face making her heart flutter and pick up speed. But there was tension around his eyes. He settled beside them and rested his head on her other leg, facing his sleeping child. The thick strands of his hair were softer since he'd started using the conditioner she'd given him. "Did the new molding fit?"

"Not yet. I need to make another adjustment. Old houses like this are rarely level or plum." He smoothed curls away from his daughter's cheek. "What were you all looking at on the ground earlier?"

"A fairy," she said and laughed at his skeptical cocked-brow expression. "It was a little gopher poking his head out of a hole."

He sat up, and with their fingers laced, he kissed her hand, and she caught the flash of passion in his eyes. Something was different about the way he looked at her. Deep. Searching. And it made her tingle in all the right places, especially her heart.

"Have you finished the designs you want to send?" he asked.

"Not yet. They can't be just good, they have to be great." If she wanted Loren Lane to choose her designs, which she very much did, she had to send her best work.

"You don't want to miss the deadline."

"I won't."

Lilly stretched and sat up. "Hi, Daddy. You sleepy, too?"

"No. I was just watching you sleep. Are you hungry? I'm so hungry I could eat ten hamburgers."

Lilly held up both hands with her fingers splayed. "This many?"

"Yep," he said.

She shook her head and wagged her finger. "No, no, no. You will get a tummy ache."

"Can I have two?"

"Okay." She held up one finger on each hand. "Two hamburger."

Jenny hugged her sweet girl and let happiness surround her. "I think I will only have one."

Brad stood up and shook himself before coming around to put his head on Eric's lap. "I think this guy is hungry, too."

As they gathered everything up to go inside, Jenny put Lilly on her hip. "I called Mimi and told her about what we found. Next time she comes over, she wants to go into the secret passageway. But she's the only person I've told. I don't think we should let too many people know about it."

"I don't either."

"I am tempted to tell Anson just so I can say I told you so."

"Toad you so," Lilly said and clapped her hands as she repeated the phrase.

Eric chuckled. "I trust him, and I would love to see you tell him he was wrong about there being a secret passageway."

Eric spent his days working with his new construction crew, playing with Lilly, working on the Christmas list and, even though he knew it was foolish, living like the three of them were a family. His nights with Jenny were spent as lovers and friends. And he fell deeper in love every day. Preparing himself for her to leave would be way more difficult than he'd ever anticipated.

On this cozy evening, a movie played on the TV, he read a new detective novel and the three of them sat on the couch with Lilly snuggled between them. Eric's contentment and sense of peace was starting to feel…normal, and not like some wishful dream. His little girl thrived in their new home and that was due in part to the beautiful woman who fit in their lives like a missing piece. Rather than paying attention to the movie, Jenny worked on a fancy dress in her sketchbook. She sighed, ripped out the drawing and crumpled it into a ball.

Eric had watched her do this over the last week. She'd work and rework her designs, never thinking they were good enough. This made him realize how anxious he was for her to send her work to Loren Lane. Against his better judgment, he hoped a little more each day that she'd have a reason not to go away to school at all. Selfish but true.

He rubbed his eyes. *These are things I never thought I'd wish for.*

"What was wrong with that drawing?" he asked.

"It's just not right. It has to be better. Something special and different that will stand out from everything else."

"Why don't you send the designs you've made for kids and the adaptive clothing? Those are different."

"I do love making kid's clothes, but that's not the kind of thing they will want. I've looked at their website, and they don't have a children's line."

Lilly shook her finger at Jenny. "No lines. I not like lines."

They chuckled and shared a smile over her head.

"I don't like standing in line either," Jenny said.

"We're not talking about the kind of lines we had to stand in when we lived in Chicago, Lilly Bug."

"Your daddy is talking about the clothes I've made for you and Hannah and Cody."

"Okay." Happy with that answer, she went back to watching her movie.

Eric put his arm across the back of the couch and massaged Jenny's neck. "I think all of your stuff is really nice."

"You have to say that because you're my boyfriend." She sucked in a breath and shot him a startled wide-eyed look. "Did I just freak you out by saying that? It just came out."

His blood pressure didn't rise. In fact, his heart rate beat at a steady pace. "No. I like being called your boyfriend." And he meant it. But he resisted professing his love. "Think the rumors will die down if you call me your boyfriend in town?"

She laughed. "Not a chance."

The next day, Jenny and Lilly went to see Mimi, and since Jenny had used his computer, he easily found the information he needed and called Loren Lane. After asking to speak to someone about the call for new designers, he waited on hold for several minutes before a woman came on the line.

"Hello. This is Loren."

He hadn't expected to talk to Loren Lane herself. He hadn't even been sure anyone would talk to him at all. "Hi. I'm Eric McKnight."

"I hear that you have some questions about designs you'd like to send?"

"Yes, but I'm not the designer. I want to know if I can submit something on behalf of someone else who doesn't believe her designs are good enough? It's my daughter's nanny. Everyone, including other seamstresses, think she's extremely talented." He purposely did not call Jenny his girlfriend because he figured Mrs. Lane would take it more seriously if she didn't know he was in love with her.

"Well, there's nothing in the rules against you sending them. What kind of designs are they?"

"They're for adaptive clothing for children, but since I understand you don't have a children's line, I'm sure they could be made into adult designs." Unable to remains seated, he walked circles around the library as he talked.

"Actually, we have been seriously considering adding a children's line. Tell me more about the adaptive clothing."

"They are not only practical, they're super cute, too. She makes clothes for lots of kids and adults in town and has been for years. They come to her with special orders, and she makes one-of-a-kind clothes," Eric continued and told her about Lilly's unique needs and how Jenny's designs had helped, the other adaptive items she'd made and how much her talent could help others with unique challenges.

"You have me very intrigued, Mr. McKnight. I'd love to see them."

There was laughter in the background, making him think it might be a place Jenny would fit in. "If I send the kids designs, can she still send you her fancy stuff?"

She chuckled then cleared her throat. "Yes. If a boss is this excited about her designs, then I'd love to see it all."

"That's great." He wrote down what he needed to do and thanked her. And before they hung up, he mentioned Jenny's dedication, strong work ethic and passion for sewing.

Once he hung up, he felt good about his decision to send everything Loren had told him. If nothing came of it then no harm done. But if they loved them as much as he thought they would, it would be a nice surprise for Jenny. And selfishly, it could be good for him and Lilly as well. In his opinion, what she was doing was important and needed to be out in the world now, and not after years of school. People needed what she had to offer them.

Before his girls got home, he made color copies from Jenny's sketchbook and pulled a few photos from his phone that showed Lilly wearing the clothes. He'd put them in the mail soon. Now he had to figure out how to get clothing samples to send and hope she didn't notice.

His gut was telling him that Jenny wanted to stay in Texas, and maybe even Oak Hollow, and that maybe she loved him, too. And he'd learned to trust his gut.

Jenny and Mimi's house was cozy, and as Eric had expected, decorated for Christmas from top to bottom. Stockings were hung across the fireplace mantel, and there was even one for the grandfather she'd lost several years ago. He picked up a photo of Jenny as a child, grinning from ear to ear while standing under a tree loaded with peaches.

"Everything is ready to decorate our gingerbread

houses," Jenny said and held out a red apron with the words *The Grinch who loved Christmas*. "I made this just for you."

He wanted to kiss her but settled for squeezing her hand. He'd never worn an apron in his life, but Jenny had a way of getting him to try new things. And he liked it. "Thank you. Are you still determined to turn me into Mr. Christmas?"

"I sure am. And I think it's working." She gave him a quick kiss, put the apron over his head and tied the strings.

"Daddy, you come now," Lilly called from the kitchen.

"I'm coming." He wrapped his arm around Jenny's shoulders, and they joined Lilly and Mimi in the kitchen. The table was covered with bowls of brightly colored candy and tubes of frosting.

Eric couldn't take his eyes from Jenny as she held Lilly around the waist, and they decorated her gingerbread house. She kissed his child's curls, and the look Jenny gave her was more than her mother ever had. It was the way a mother should look at her child. He had vague fuzzy memories of his own mother looking at him with love, but he was never sure if they were real memories or wishful daydreams. Jenny caught him staring and smiled. A smile that made his chest warm then tighten.

Mimi handed him a tube of white frosting. "You get to put on the almond and pretzel shingles. And don't even try to tell me you don't know how to do it."

"Yes, ma'am." Mimi treated him like part of the family, and it felt nice. "I do have some experience when it comes to shingles."

When it was time to put on the final touches, Lilly chose two gingerbread people to put in front of the house. "They always live together. This is daddy gingeeman and Lilly." She placed them next to the front door and Jenny helped her secure them into place with a bit of frosting. Lilly held up a third cookie. "This is Jenny. You are the mommy gingee-bread." Lilly put the cookie beside the others and hugged her nanny.

Jenny and Eric locked eyes over his daughter's head, and his heart banged behind his rib cage like a hammer on a nail. His daughter wanted the same thing he did. This amazing woman to be in their lives.

While Jenny took Lilly outside to see where she had played as a child, Eric and Mimi sat on the front porch with cups of coffee. Not for the first time, Eric considered talking to Jenny about the possibility of attending a school that wasn't so far from Oak Hollow. He'd even researched design schools in Texas, the closest only a few hours away. There had been no words about the designs he'd sent on her behalf, and he checked his email daily, anxious to know where their relationship could go if she was offered a job. Even though Dallas was a big city, he'd consider moving there if it meant being with her.

"Has Jenny always been interested in sewing and making clothes and fashion stuff?"

Mimi chuckled. "Since she was a little girl. She used to design clothes for her dolls and ask me to make them. She'd sit beside me and watch, and then I started teaching her. She picked up the skills quickly and became an excellent seamstress at a young age. And now, people come to her all of the time to make something special."

Eric put his coffee cup on the small table between them. "Even I can see her talent."

"She started talking about becoming a fashion designer when she was in the fifth grade."

"So, it's been her dream?"

"Yes." Mimi plucked a dried leaf from a hanging basket. "She has worked long and hard toward this goal, including putting it on hold to take care of me through cancer treatments. And without my knowledge, she used the money she'd saved to pay for some of the medical bills. I was too sick at the time to realize what she'd done."

He watched Jenny settle on a swing hanging in a front yard tree with Lilly on her lap. "That sounds like something she would do. How is your health now?"

"It's good. I'm cancer-free." She reached across the table and put a gentle hand on his arm. "You care about my granddaughter, don't you?"

"Sure." He waved to the girls, and the warmth of

love filled him. "She's great with my daughter, and Lilly will really miss her."

"And you? Will you miss her, too?"

Her knowing expression told him there was no hiding his feelings from this smart woman. But he did not need to let her know the depths of those feelings. With a galloping pulse beating at his chest and throat, he answered, "Yes. You know better than anyone what a good heart she has. Is there anyone who doesn't like her?"

"I can't think of anyone." The wind blew her hair across her cheek and she tucked it behind her ear.

"I have an idea for a Christmas present for Jenny. Do you happen to know who bought all of Mrs. Barton's snow globes at the estate sale?"

"I know who ran the sale. And I bet she has a record of it."

"I'm hoping to buy some of them back if possible."

Mimi smiled. "That's a beautiful idea. I'll call my friend after y'all leave."

Brad bounded onto the porch, sat at Eric's feet and leaned against his knee. "He's telling me he's hungry. I guess I better get him and my girls home."

Oh shoot. I just called them my girls out loud.

Chapter Eighteen

Jenny sat on the foot of Lilly's bed, watching her stretch like she always did when waking up, and she remembered what it was like to be a kid on Christmas morning. When she glanced at Eric, her heart ached for the magical Christmas mornings he hadn't experienced, but seeing the way he smiled at his daughter, she knew this one would be special.

"Lilly Bug, are you ready to get up?" he said and kissed her forehead.

She rubbed her eyes. "Daddy, is it Christmas yet?"

"Yes," Eric said. "Want to go see what Santa brought?"

"Yes, yes, yes." Suddenly wide awake, Lilly clapped and bounced on the bed.

He lifted her high into the air until she giggled, and then he cuddled her close.

Jenny wrapped her arms around them. "Merry Christmas." Resting her head on Eric's chest and returning Lilly's beaming smile filled her with so much love she thought she'd burst.

"Merry Christmas to my beautiful girls." He kissed each of them. "This is going to be a great day." With Lilly on his hip, he took Jenny's hand, and led her down the hallway.

"Mimi is in the living room, and she's ready to take a video as we come in," she said to Eric. "I think you should go in first and that way you can see Lilly's reaction."

He shifted his daughter into her arms. "That's a nice idea."

Lilly tossed her head back. "Let's go-o-o. It's Christmas."

They chuckled, and Eric kissed them again before going in ahead of them.

"Lilly, do you want me to carry you or do you want to walk?"

"I want to walk." She wiggled to get down.

Jenny took both of her hands. "Here we come," she called out so Mimi would be ready with her camera.

Lilly's delighted gasp brought true happiness to Eric's face, and that alone was worth every bit of effort it had taken to get him to go along with the Christmas list idea.

Colorfully wrapped boxes and toys from Santa made an impressive display. Lilly hugged the big stuffed dog that looked a lot like Brad, who was currently sniffing the bone tied with a red bow. In their matching Christmas pajamas, they all four sat on the floor in front of the tree and the gift opening began.

Lilly climbed onto Jenny's lap and handed her a small flat box wrapped in silver paper. "For you."

"Oh goodie. Will you help me open it?" They each tore away some of the paper, and she lifted the lid. A silver charm bracelet was nestled on the padding with two charms. A sewing machine and a fairy. "This is so gorgeous. Thank you so much, sweet girl. Did you pick out the fairy?"

"Yep. And Daddy pick that one." Lilly wrapped her arms around Jenny's neck. "I wuv you."

"I love you, too." She held her tighter, soaking in every bit of sweetness she could. How had this little one completely stolen her heart? When she caught Eric watching them, she thought she saw him wipe away a tear.

"I think this one is for my Lilly Bug," he said and slid a gift her way.

"Wow. Big one." She clapped then crooked her finger at Mimi. "You can help me?"

"I'd love to." Mimi settled the little girl on her lap and laughed when Lilly tossed the sparkly green bow high into the air.

Jenny loved seeing the smile on her grandmother's face and the healthy glow back in her cheeks. She didn't think the day could get much better, until she saw the row of snow globes on the mantel beside the fairy that Eric had carved for Lilly. "Oh my goodness. Where did these come from?" She rushed to the fireplace. A big red tag was nestled between two of them. *To Jenny From Eric.* She spun to face him. "Thank you so much. How did you find these?"

He wrapped his arms around her from behind and kissed her cheek. "I had a little help from Mimi."

Her grandmother smiled at them. "I didn't do much. It was this young man who got it done."

"This is such a wonderful gift."

"I'm glad they make you happy. Thank you for making this the best Christmas ever."

"I saw you unwrap the books, but you haven't opened my other present for you." She left the comfort of his arms to grab a package from under the tree.

"'To Mr. Christmas,'" Eric read and then laughed. "You have accomplished your mission, fairy woman."

"Then you'll like what's inside this box."

He sat on the couch and pulled out the scrapbook she'd been putting together. Flipping open the cover, he chuckled. Although it was a bit tattered from use, stained with frosting and smudged fingerprints, *Lilly's Christmas List* was on the first page. They reminisced as they looked through the timeline of their days together.

Jenny pointed to a shot of Eric and Lilly in the store buying decorations. "This photo is from the early days of the list. That expression on your face is priceless."

"I do look a little grumpy in that one." He laughed, and it sounded more like Santa than the Grinch.

She had written captions for each photo and included other mementos like the ribbon they'd won at the cookie contest. The pages showed Eric's transition to Mr. Christmas.

The delightful aroma of freshly baked cinnamon rolls and coffee reached them before Mimi returned to the room with a loaded tray. "Who's hungry?"

"Me," Lilly cheered and clapped. "I want yummies."

Wrapping paper, ribbons and sparkly tissue paper were spread across half of the room. While Lilly played with her new toys by the tree, and Mimi chatted on the phone with Joseph, they just enjoyed being with one another. They spent the entire day in their pajamas, eating, playing and savoring their time together.

In the early evening, Mimi left for a date with Joseph, and it was just the three of them again. Snuggling on the couch with soft music and a crackling fire was Jenny's idea of the best Christmas night ever.

The scrapbook was on the coffee table, and Eric flipped it open to the first page. "This is a perfect Christmas list. It led me step by step to you. I've been searching for a home my whole life, and you've helped me turn this house into a home."

She pressed her hand to her heart, and a lovely feeling of lightness filled her. She wanted to be part of his home. Part of their family. And resting her head on his chest she was right where she wanted to be. "This house is ready for a lot more memories." And she hoped to be a part of those memories.

Eric shifted to smile at his daughter, curled up and sleeping beside the Christmas tree with her faithful dog. The tenderness in his expression sent a surge of love and longing to Jenny's core, and she almost opened her mouth to tell him she would stay in Oak Hollow.

Not yet. I promised myself I would not make a final decision until after *this trip.* Tomorrow she'd go to New York City, and maybe by the time she got back, she'd hear something about the designs she'd submitted to Loren Lane.

Her heart was strongly leaning in one direction. But what if she got there and her excitement was renewed? Maybe she'd realize she needed to at least give it a shot. She could not let herself later regret her decision or feel like she'd passed up something important.

The sun was barely peeking over the horizon, but Eric couldn't go back to sleep. Not with the woman he loved nestled against his side. Inhaling her sweet floral scent into his lungs, he trailed his fingers over the length of her back, loving the way she arched into his touch. Jenny was leaving on her trip today, and he had a feeling this would be a deciding moment for them.

She kissed his bare chest and met his gaze with a sleepy smile. "Good morning."

"Morning, beautiful. Are you excited about your trip?"

"I'm excited and nervous."

I'm nervous, too. He smoothed his hand along her silky hair. "Why are you nervous?"

Propped up on her elbow, she sighed. "I'm not sure. It just feels like something important is around the corner. What can I bring you from New York City?"

"Only one thing. You." His heart clattered against his breastbone. It was the truth, but maybe he shouldn't have said it out loud.

"I can do that."

This time she'd come back. But the next… She couldn't promise him that she would. "What time is Alexandra picking you up?"

"Nine o'clock. And I'm all packed, so I don't have to get up yet. Lilly is not awake. Want to close the door and show me how much you're going to miss me?"

"I can also do that. With pleasure." He rolled out of bed, peeked in to check on Lilly, then closed and locked the door. "I've never been more thankful for thick solid wood doors."

Eric braced his hands on the door frame between his and Lilly's rooms. Jenny moved with her usual grace from the closet to the dresser, and he couldn't take his eyes off her. Who would've thought that watching her doing something as simple and everyday as putting away laundry could make him so happy? Four nights without her wouldn't be so bad.

She smiled and tossed a pair of his socks, and he caught them with ease.

He should stop telling himself lies. Four nights were four too many. Missing her was a given. Was he wrong to hope she would hate the city and be eager to rush back home to him and Lilly?

She closed the top dresser drawer. "Have you seen the wrap pants I made for Lilly? The ones with Velcro for easy access to her new brace? I thought they were in the pile of laundry I've been putting off doing, but they weren't. I also can't find the shirt samples I made for port and G-tube access."

He'd known there was a high chance of this happening, and he should've told her what he'd done. But he'd put it off in hopes that they'd hear from Loren Lane before Jenny found out. Eric shoved his hands in his back pockets and stepped forward.

"I took them."

"Where'd you put them?" She glanced around the room.

"In the mail."

"In the what?" Her head tilted as her eyes widened.

He'd never seen her mad but had a feeling that was about to change. It might be time to pay up for his screwup. "I put them in the mail with copies of your sketches. To Loren Lane."

Her mouth dropped open then snapped into a hard line. "You. Did. What?"

Her words were slow and loaded with enough ammunition to flatten him, and he could hear blood rushing in his ears. *Yep. Big trouble.* "They know it wasn't you who sent them. Ten days before Christmas I sent them on your behalf with photos of Lilly."

"But..." She paced across the room. "Those aren't the things I wanted to send. Not at all what I planned."

"I know. That's why I sent them. I called and they—"

"Eric! It's not the impression I needed to make to have any chance at..." She lowered her head and rubbed her forehead before meeting his gaze. "You can't interfere in my career like this. Do you do this to every woman in your life?"

Her words hit with the force of a flash-bang grenade. Déjà vu of the worst kind. His legs went numb and he sat on the bed. He could still hear Lilly's mother yelling that he needed to stay out of her business. That he had no right to tell her what to do. That he was holding her back from her career. Celia's plan to leave their brand-new baby had been too reminiscent of his own childhood. He'd only been trying to protect his daughter and give her the kind of childhood that had been stolen from him.

But a few hours later, he'd been left alone to raise Lilly.

Out of fear and anger, he'd made demands and angered Cilia enough to leave in the middle of the night. And die on the way to the airport. A cold chill skidded down his spine. It was his fault Lilly didn't have a mother.

And now, in his eagerness for Jenny to stay, he'd done the same thing. *Why didn't I learn my lesson?*

"Eric, are you even listening to me?"

He rubbed his face, trying to erase the past. The memories that haunted him. The guilt. "I'm sorry, Jenny. I really am."

"You know what?" She closed her eyes and took a deep breath. "We'll have to finish this discussion later. Alexandra will be here any minute." She didn't look at him, just spun away and left the bedroom.

Anxiety wound into a tight knot in his gut. Interfering in her plans had been a foolish move. He should go after her and explain his reason for sending her designs without permission, but now he was second-guessing his decision to bring her into their lives on a permanent basis. Not because she was mad at him, but because he couldn't risk a repeat of what happened with Cilia.

He pulled his sorry butt up off the bed and made his way to the living room where Lilly played, but he stayed out of sight and listened to them talk.

"I have to go on my trip now, sweet girl."

"No. You stay, Fairy Jenny."

His little girl's words echoed his wish, and he almost stepped into the room, but uncertainty held him back. *I know better than to make a wish.*

"I'll be back soon, and I'll bring you a surprise. Be good for your daddy."

"I wuv you."

"I love you too, sweetie. Give me a big, big hug so it will last me until I get back."

And now he was gutted. How long would a hug or kiss need to be to last when she moved? With a heart that was already breaking, he realized what he needed to prepare for. There would be no Eric and Jenny building a family together in Oak Hollow. She'd do her thing across the country, and he'd continue to power through just as he always did.

The tension in his chest became painful as the wheels of Jenny's suitcase rattled across the wooden floor and the front door closed.

Where do I go from here?

"Daddy, where a-a-are you?"

I go to my daughter. "I'm here, Lilly Bug. Daddy will always be here."

Chapter Nineteen

Jenny rolled her suitcase across the uneven bricks of Eric's front walk, breathing deeply to calm herself. She'd worked so hard on her designs. Trying to make them perfect, with just the right touch of class and an unexpected twist. Not to mention wishing on stars and crossing her fingers that her designs would be so well received it would be the proof she could make it in this profession without a degree.

A sinking feeling weighed her down. She'd sent her package only three days ago. So the designs she'd so carefully chosen would not be their first impression of her skills. It would be what Eric had sent.

Alexandra pulled up in her little sports car, waved and popped the trunk. With her suitcase stowed, Jenny settled into the front passenger side. "Good morning."

With one look, her friend picked up on her mood. "Oh no, what happened?"

"I have a man-shaped problem."

Alexandra laughed and turned the car around. "You were happy when I called earlier. What went wrong in the last hour?"

"He sent designs for my adaptive clothing to Loren Lane without asking me."

Alexandra turned down the radio. "Hmm. Why do you think he did it?"

"I have no idea. He said he sent them because I wouldn't. Three days ago, I mailed the designs I've been working on for weeks. He was with me and didn't say one word about what he'd done." As they zipped along the curving road, she took in the sight of wide-open space between the hills, the river and grazing animals. Breathing deeply, she tried to calm down and think.

"I do know that he's proud of you," Alexandra said. "When you came over for dinner, he told me how much it means to him that you are making clothes to help families like his."

The ache in her chest became a knot in her stomach. "Really? Now I feel bad about leaving without a proper goodbye." *And kiss.* She glanced out the back window. They were already too far away to go back and still make their flight. And it was probably best if she took some time to calm down and think clearly before talking to him.

When she'd freaked out about what he'd done, Eric had thrown up a wall between them. She'd felt it, especially when his face paled. Jenny knew why she was mad, but had an uneasy feeling something she'd said had caused him to revert to the quiet man she'd first met.

Yelling at him and then leaving hadn't been her

best idea, but she'd panicked that he'd ruined her one shot at a responsible excuse to stay.

The taxi ride from the airport was terrifying and thrilling. The city was enormous both from the air and submerged in its depths, like a thick forest of glass, metal and stone. She couldn't stop smiling as they passed landmarks she'd seen only in movies and almost gave herself whiplash trying to see everything at once. When they got to Uncle Leo's and Aunt Sari's house and saw the garage apartment, it was adorable. But just as Alexandra had warned, it was so tiny. A far cry from the Barton Estate.

And a long way from Lilly and Eric.

She enjoyed sightseeing, excellent food and attending the wedding with Alexandra. Everyone raved over their dresses. And her friend proudly told everyone that Jenny had designed and made them.

The morning of their last day, Alexandra was taking her to visit the school she'd dreamed of attending for so many years. At the top of a stairway leading down into the subway station, Jenny paused at the view below. A sea of people in dark coats moved swiftly, shoulder to shoulder, reminding her of a rushing river. Alexandra chuckled, took her by the arm and led her down the stairs. Was this the kind of crowd that had turned Eric off to city life? She kept hold of her friend until they were seated on the train.

Jenny scooted closer to Alexandra so a woman

could sit beside her. "Wow, this is a lot of people in one place. Good thing I'm not claustrophobic."

"It's not always this crowded. We hit right at the worst possible day and time. You'll get used to it. And just keep in mind that you won't get the full picture of what school will be like since so many students are away for the holidays."

"That's what the lady said on the phone. But there are some students there working on projects." The train rhythmically swayed and lights flickered as they zipped along the tracks. "This is how I would get to school each day?"

"Yes. Don't worry, my country friend. I'll make sure you know what to do. I'll write everything down."

At one time, there had been no question about what Jenny wanted to do with her life. But was she going after a dream that no longer fit?

"This is where we get off," Alexandra said.

The design school was a short walk from the subway station. Jenny took note of everything they passed. The people watching was one of her favorite things.

"I need coffee before I punch someone." Alexandra pointed to a cute coffee shop. "Do you want something?"

"I don't think I need any caffeine." She could see the entrance to the school just up ahead and was anxious to get there and check it out. "Will you meet me inside after you get your coffee?"

"Sure. See you in a few."

Standing in front of the school she'd dreamed of attending for so many years, Jenny waited for the excitement to kick in. There were so many possibilities. So many opportunities waiting inside. A group of girls came out onto the sidewalk, all of them smiling and talking about which bar to go to that night. Would she even fit in with them? The younger version of herself would have, but now she wasn't so sure.

She waited for a couple to pass then took a few steps toward the door, her thoughts spinning like the ballerina in her childhood jewelry box. This had been her plan for so long she couldn't remember why she wanted to go so far away to such a massive city. A decision she'd made when she was so much younger and a different person. She'd been a teenager who wanted to know what was out there. Wanted to get out of her hometown and have an adventure.

Something bubbled inside her, but it was not enthusiasm to walk through these doors and become a student. It was love. All she could think about was holding Lilly and hearing her sweet voice. Kissing Eric and feeling safe with his strong arms wrapped around her.

And all she wanted to do was go home to Oak Hollow.

Alexandra walked up beside her and followed her line of vision to the front double doors. "Why haven't you gone inside?"

“Is it giving up if I decide not to go to school?”

Her friend’s smile broadened. “No. It’s definitely not giving up.”

“I was waiting and hoping to hear from Loren Lane, but I know what I want. I want to stay in Oak Hollow and continue the life I already have.”

“What took you so long? We’ve known this for months and have been waiting for you to realize it.” Alexandra hooked her arm through Jenny’s and pulled her along. “Eric and Lilly will be as happy as we are that you are staying.”

As they walked, Jenny’s steps suddenly felt lighter. “It’s been coming for a while, but I needed to be here for myself and see.”

Alexandra motioned to a bench and they sat. “I wasn’t supposed to tell you this until you made your decision, but Tess wants to offer you a space to set up some of your clothes in her new antiques shop on the square.”

“Really?” She drummed her fingers on her thighs. Ideas forming. “I also got an offer to have a space in Emma’s Vintage.”

“That’s my favorite store,” Alexandra said. “Luke tries to keep us on the other side of the square so I won’t see what’s new in the window.”

Jenny laughed. “I know. He told me. And so did Cody.” She pulled out the pro-and-con list from her purse and unfolded it. “This list should’ve given me my answer weeks ago, but I had to be sure. Reasons to go to school has three positive things. It's the plan, career opportunities and adventure."

Alexandra leaned closer to study the wrinkled paper. "And you have ten reasons to stay in Oak Hollow. Mimi won't be alone. Won't miss Lilly growing up. Eric, with a heart beside his name." She grinned and continued to read the list. "Awe, I'm on your reasons to stay list."

"Of course you are. Good friends are priceless. I have everything I need at home. I can continue making clothes for people in the Texas Hill Country. And even if I never design for a fashion house, I have a life I love."

"And a sweet little girl and her hot dad."

"True. Lilly's birthday is in February, and I don't want to miss it or any of her birthdays." *Or a single day without either of them.* "Do you think Eric sent my designs because he wants me to stay?"

Her friend laughed. "Um, yes!"

Jenny had been gone for only a few days, and his house felt too big, his bed too empty and like something was missing. He'd gone back and forth a hundred times about the right thing to do where Jenny was concerned.

Needing fresh air and a change of scenery, Eric put Lilly in the sandbox he'd built in the backyard and tossed a tennis ball for Brad. This New York City trip was a sharp reminder of what it would be like when she left for good. It didn't feel like she'd gone on a trip, it felt like she'd left *him*. He shook his head and tossed the tennis ball harder than necessary. Jenny wasn't leaving him. She'd been planning to go long before he showed up in Oak Hollow to start over.

Lilly's sweet voice carried on the breeze as she sang "Jingle Bells." So happy and carefree while playing in the sand. His job was to do everything in his power to protect her. Even if that meant denying himself the love he'd found. If he encouraged Jenny to stay in Oak Hollow or switch schools, he'd be risking not only his heart this time but also his daughter's. He had allowed himself to believe Jenny might change her mind and stay in Oak Hollow, but he couldn't shake up their whole world for something that wasn't a sure thing.

At some point Jenny might get anxious or dissatisfied and realize she'd given up something important. She'd leave them because he'd held her back. And he did not want to do that dance again. He loved Jenny enough that he didn't want that for her either.

"I can't risk our hearts on a maybe." *Maybe she'll come home to Oak Hollow. Maybe she'll love me forever.* But there was no maybe about the heartache to come.

The responsible thing to do was think of the future, both for himself and his girls. He wanted her to stay with them, but if it wasn't best for Jenny, then it was no good for him and Lilly. When Cilia left them it was horrible, but if Jenny stayed only to discover she wanted to leave later, it might kill him.

Brad trotted over to stretch out in a patch of sunshine, and Eric knelt to rub his head.

"I cannot let her become a major part of our lives only to have her change her mind when she realizes the opportunity she passed up."

Brad gave a big doggie sigh and rolled over for a tummy scratch.

"You said it, boy." They couldn't keep going the way they were, living as a family and pretending it wouldn't end. But how in the world was he supposed to end a relationship that felt so right?

Chapter Twenty

Jenny had a camera filled with tons of fabulous photos and hoped to visit New York City again, but her life was in Oak Hollow. And she couldn't wait to get started on the next phase. Even though she was the one who loved snow globes, she'd bought one for Eric with the New York City skyline. She'd tell him it was a reminder of the time she went to New York and decided her future.

When Alexandra dropped her off at Eric's house, she was both excited and nervous. Her love for him was not a question, and even though he'd never said the words, she was betting on his love. Entering through the kitchen door, she heard Lilly singing in the living room and made her way there, still holding all of her bags. Her sweet girl was dressed in her fairy pajamas and coloring at the coffee table with Brad beside her.

"My Fairy Jenny's back," Lilly squealed and started crawling toward her.

"Hello, my sweet girl." She set down her bags and hugged the child she'd grown to love like her own. "I missed you." The dog barked and rubbed his head against her. "And I missed you too, good boy."

"You bring me a surprise?"

"I did." Jenny chuckled, reached into her carry-on and pulled out a doll that Lilly immediately hugged and started playing with.

When Jenny glanced over her shoulder, Eric was standing behind her with wet hair and a blank expression. She smiled, but he did not smile back. And her heart stuttered behind her ribs. He looked sad. Like the old Eric. The stoic man she'd met on day one. She kissed Lilly's cheek then walked toward him, wanting to be held and kissed, but he did not uncross his arms or say a word. Was he mad about the way she'd left?

"Eric, I'm so sorry I left the way I did. I should not have gone while we were arguing. Shouldn't have left without kissing you."

"It's not that." He inhaled deeply and motioned for her to follow him out of the room, and she knew something bad was coming.

Her stomach roiled and tossed as she followed him to the library. "You're scaring me. What's wrong?"

"I figured I should start the search and was surprised to find someone so quickly, but..." He shrugged and stared at his feet. "It's best that we don't prolong the inevitable."

An uncomfortable knot formed in her throat. "What are you talking about?"

"A new nanny. I'll still pay you for the time agreed on, but I've hired another nanny. She can start right away."

Ice formed in her core and pierced something inside her. Speechless and stunned, she just stared at him. *He replaced me? Already?* She shook her head and found her voice. "What if I want to keep the job?"

He met her eyes fully for the first time since she'd come home. "You are going to New York, and you are going to school."

"You do not get to make that decision for me." Now she was hurt *and* angry. Her fists clenched and she walked toward him, not sure if she was going to smack him or take his hand and see if she could bring back the man she loved.

Everything rattled on the desk as he bumped it in his retreat. "But I get to make the decision of what's best for me and Lilly. And this is the best choice."

"What was all the time we spent together? Did it mean nothing to you?"

"It was fun, and I'll always have good memories, but life goes on. We always knew it was…short-term."

"Fun?" *That's what he has to say about our time together?*

He shrugged and ducked his head. "I'm not built for long-term relationships."

Her lungs constricted, making each breath a chore, and she sat on the chair in front of the fireplace before her legs gave out. Could he so easily put her aside and move on? Is this what his childhood had taught him to do?

"I think it's best for Lilly if you say goodbye to

her now and not wait until… Waiting will only make it harder."

How could this get harder? Her heart was shattering. "You're asking me to leave tonight?"

"You can put her to bed before you go. I've already reminded her that you were never going to be here forever."

Forever. Just when forever was what she wanted with them. How had she been so wrong? If he could so easily do this, then maybe he wasn't the man she'd thought he was. When she just stared at him, blinking to hold back tears, he looked away and walked to the door as if they were done talking, but he stopped.

"I won't keep you from seeing Lilly. She can come over and visit at your house. When you're home."

"I…" She inhaled and tried to make sense of the shock she'd come back to. A major wrinkle in her new life plan. At least he wasn't planning to keep Lilly from seeing her. There was no reason to punish her because her father was being a heartless jerk.

"I'll go get your check."

She stabbed a finger at him. "You're being an ass."

"It's not the first time I've been called that." With his blank expression, he turned and walked away. Dragging her heart behind him.

She was too shocked to cry, and that was good because she didn't want Lilly to see her sobbing. With her best happy face in place, she gathered up her sweet girl, helped her brush her teeth and read two books before she fell asleep. Jenny lay beside her, stroking her soft curls and watching her sleep. She kissed her one more time then hugged Brad.

She braced herself to see Eric, but when she came out of Lilly's room, her purse was sitting on top of her suitcase with a check sticking out of the side pocket. It was for the coming weeks. The weeks that he didn't want her around. But she didn't want his money—that was probably only to make himself feel better about what he'd done. And now she was even angrier. She ripped the check in two and put it on the kitchen counter by the coffee pot. Packing the rest of her things would have to wait for another day.

On the drive home, the tears came in a flood of emotion, and she had to pull over on the side of the road. Eric's crappy new attitude was not going to stop her from staying in Oak Hollow. Her mind was made up, and it was the right decision for her.

But being dismissed so callously was heartbreaking.

I guess he's not the man I thought he was.

Mimi looked up from her needlework. "Hello, sweetheart." Her grandmother's smile fell away, and she jumped up to pull her into her arms. "What's wrong?"

"He hired another nanny and dismissed me like there was never anything between us. Like I was just some random employee."

Mimi stroked her head like she'd done when Jenny was little. "Let's sit and you can tell me what happened."

They sat in their favorite comfy chairs and settled in for one of their talks. "Eric's pushing me away, and I'm not sure why."

Jenny told her everything and they both cried, some tears for her and a few for him.

Eric never cried. Hadn't since he was a child, but tears rolled down his cheeks and he let them fall. The tension in his chest made him wonder if he was having a heart attack. Had he just made a huge mistake?

He rubbed his eyes and turned to go check on his daughter, but with his vision blurred, he brushed against the Christmas tree. A glittery ball fell off and shattered but he caught the second one. He looked at the wish ornament in his hand. The one Jenny had insisted he make. The one he hadn't put a wish in. Was that why things had ended like this? Because he hadn't made a wish?

Christmas was over, but it was still December. Maybe Christmas wishes could still be granted. He didn't know exactly what to wish for but hoped it would come to him when he unrolled the blank piece of paper from his ornament. He got a pair of tweezers from his bathroom then sat on his bed. Once the top hanger was removed, he pulled out the slip of red paper. But when he unrolled it, there were words on the paper, and his heart skipped a beat.

Lilly wants Jenny to be her mommy.

This wasn't his, it was his daughter's wish. His stomach roiled and he had to lean forward to keep from being sick. He was too late. His and Lilly's hearts already belonged to Jenny. But was it too late to make things right after what he'd just done to the woman he loved? Would she forgive him?

He put Lilly's ornament back together and walked to the living room to rehang it on the tree. He was tempted to see what wish was in Jenny's ornament, but that seemed wrong.

Making sure he had his ornament, he opened it. For several minutes he just stared at the paper, trying to come up with a wish that would make everyone happy. Options rolled through his head. He finally picked up a pencil and wrote down his late Christmas wish.

I want happiness for everyone that I love.

His phone rang and Anson's number appeared on the screen. He didn't feel like talking to anyone, but what if something had happened to Jenny on the way home? With his pulse racing, he answered. "Hello."

"I heard the good news," his buddy said in a cheery voice.

"What news?"

"That Jenny decided to stay in Oak Hollow and not go to school."

"What?" He shot to his feet.

"Um… Isn't she there with you?"

"She was, but..." He mumbled a string of colorful curse words. "I screwed up bad."

"Tell me."

He told Anson what he'd done, sparing a few of the details.

"Bro, I wish you had talked to me first. But it's not hopeless. Luke did something similar. We can fix this. Women love it when you make a grand gesture. Tomorrow will ring in a new year, and I can't think of a better time to grovel at her feet and let her know how much you love her. Any ideas what you can do?"

Eric looked at her stack of Christmas CDs. "I have an idea."

Jenny stood in Alexandra and Luke's backyard, decorated for New Year's Eve with gold stars and metallic streamers. The sun slipped behind the trees as happy people laughed, ate, drank and enjoyed music. Almost everyone she cared about was here or on their way. Except Eric and Lilly. She was trying to put on a happy face, but it was hard. Maybe her glass of wine would help.

She'd had time to get past some of the shock of Eric's behavior, and she recognized it was probably a self-protective measure going back to early childhood. For weeks, or more like months, she'd thought long and hard, agonizing over her decision, and if he had just listened to why she'd made a new life plan, maybe they could've figured things out. Was he too broken for her to truly reach his heart? Was her love not enough to heal some of his pain? Her eyes stung with unshed tears, and she took a large gulp of wine.

Hannah ran across the yard with streamers trailing behind her, but Cody watched the party from the safety of his treehouse, and she considered joining him.

Tess came up to her before she could make her way to the treehouse ladder. "Mimi just told me you heard from Loren Lane, but she said I had to ask you for the details."

Jenny smiled, because even though she was upset about her man-shaped problem, she really was excited about her new job. "I got the call this morning. They want me to design for their new adaptive clothing line and children's line."

"Congratulations!" Her friend's smile slipped. "Does that mean you are moving to Dallas?"

"No. That's the best part. I was brave enough to negotiate and they agreed that I can work from here and travel to Dallas a few times a month." She was wrapped in a hug and some of her wine sloshed onto the sleeve of her black sweater.

"I'm so proud of you."

"Thank you." She sighed. "And I owe it to Eric because he sent the designs that got me the job."

"Don't you think the two of you can work this out?"

She shrugged. "I'm starting to think that it was more one-sided than I realized. And maybe I shouldn't be so surprised. He did tell me that he would never marry again. And that every relationship other than being a father is temporary."

Anson joined them and put an arm around Jenny's shoulders. "I just heard from Eric, and he's decided to come after all. I didn't want it to take you by surprise."

Her heart stuttered, and she felt wound tighter than a new spool of thread. "I appreciate the heads-up. I'll have to get used to seeing him around town." Lord only knew what the rumors would be like now. She took another healthy swallow of wine. And prepared herself to see the man she loved.

Jenny was headed over to sit with Alexandra and Emma when the music turned off. Someone started singing an a cappella version of Nat King Cole's "Unforgettable." And she knew the voice. With her heart galloping, she spun around.

Eric crossed the yard with Lilly on his hip, and he was singing. In front of everyone. Lilly wore one of the dresses she'd made, and it was the first time she'd seen him in slacks and a button-up. With his heart in his eyes, he held out a hand and she took it, shivering at the touch of his skin against hers. As his amazing voice washed over her, Lilly leaned forward for a kiss, and Jenny let a happy tear slide down her cheek.

When his serenade ended, everyone cheered. It was no surprise when a blush crept across his face.

He drew her into a hug, with Lilly snuggled between them. "Can we talk?"

"Yes. I'd like that." She inhaled lavender baby

shampoo and his scent of leather and wood, and lightness filled her.

Mimi wiped away her own tears and held out her arms for Lilly. "Let's go see what Hannah is doing." She smiled at them. "She'll be fine. You two take as long as you need."

Hand in hand, she led him to Luke and Alexandra's bedroom and closed the door. "Eric, I—"

He rested a finger against her lips. "Can I go first?"

"Yes."

"Please forgive me for the horrible way I treated you. I love you, Jenny Lynn Winslet. And I should've said it sooner, but I could not risk holding you back only to have you leave us later."

His freshly shaven cheek was smooth under her hand. "I love you. And I love Lilly. And I am not leaving."

He cupped her face and kissed her softly. "Are you positive that staying here is what you want?"

"More than positive. I stood in front of the school I've wanted to attend since I was young, but I realized that I'd forgotten something very important."

"What's that?"

"My life. The people I love. The man and child who've stolen my heart."

He wrapped her in a tight embrace. "My beginning in life was rough. The middle has been a struggle with many battles and a few jagged mountains to climb. But my ending isn't written yet." He paused for a kiss and stared into her eyes. "You've found something inside me that I didn't know I had." After a deep breath, he continued, "I know this is probably way too soon, but I'm going to trust my gut. And my heart."

Eric dropped to one knee and her whole body shimmered in a wave of the most delicious chills.

"I'd like to build the rest of my life with you." Reaching into his shirt pocket, he pulled out Mrs. B's diamond ring. "Will you marry me?"

"Yes. Yes, I will." She eagerly held out her hand, and he slipped the ring onto her finger, then stood to hug her. Jenny slid her hands up to his shoulders, her lips a breath away from his. "I'd say we're already under construction, and I'm ready to build the next level."

He chuckled. "Partners in life and love?"

"You have yourself a partnership, Mr. McKnight."

"I suppose this lifetime gig comes with a pay raise."

"You can pay me in kisses because I won't be needing any of your money." Her cheeks ached, but she couldn't stop smiling. "I got a job, and I don't have to leave Oak Hollow."

"Really? Tell me."

"Thanks to you, I'll be living here and traveling to Dallas a few times a month because I'm the newest designer for Loren Lane."

He lifted her into a spinning hug. "Congratulations, fairy woman." He kissed her again, and this time it was long and slow and wonderful. "I love you."

"I'll never get tired of hearing that. I love you, too." She couldn't resist holding out her hand to admire the ring.

"I hope you don't mind that I proposed with this ring, but I thought maybe your Mrs. B would be okay with it."

"She would. It's perfect. Maybe when she said follow my dreams, she meant you and Lilly. Do you think it's possible that she really could see into the future?"

"Ordinarily, I wouldn't believe it, but this time I do," he said.

"Me, too." Happiness flowed through her like a rushing river. "Let's go find Lilly and celebrate the start of a new year." *And a new life.*

They left the bedroom, and she savored the feel of being tucked against his side once again. "I brought you a present from New York City, but I don't have it with me."

"What is it?"

"One of those cheap plastic snow globes with the city's skyline. It's to remember the time I took a trip there and made a plan for the rest of my life."

"Tell me about this plan."

"To come home to you and Lilly and the life I already have and love."

"I think I've said it before, but you have some really great ideas."

* * *

The children were asleep in Cody's room, and the adults prepared for the midnight countdown. Jenny was in her own little heaven in Eric's arms, swaying to a slow song.

"Guess what?" he whispered against her ear. "Lilly's and my Christmas wishes have come true."

"So has mine." She lifted her head from his chest. "Wait, how do you know Lilly's wish?"

He winced then laughed. "That's a story I'll tell you later. Just know that you've made me a believer in Christmas wishes." Someone started the midnight countdown. "Right now, kiss me like you want to share a life with me."

She put all of her love and desire into the kiss and was dizzy by the time he lifted his head.

He brushed her hair back from her face. "There's something else I'm looking forward to sharing with you."

"What's that?"

"My last name."

* * * * *

WE HOPE YOU ENJOYED THIS BOOK FROM

HARLEQUIN SPECIAL EDITION

Believe in love. Overcome obstacles. Find happiness.

Relate to finding comfort and strength in the support of loved ones and enjoy the journey no matter what life throws your way.

6 NEW BOOKS AVAILABLE EVERY MONTH!

HSEHALO2021

COMING NEXT MONTH FROM

HARLEQUIN

SPECIAL EDITION

#2869 THE FATHER OF HER SONS

Wild Rose Sisters • by Christine Rimmer

Easton Wright now wants to be part of his sons' lives—with the woman he fell hard for during a weeklong fling. Payton Dahl doesn't want her sons to grow up fatherless like she did, but can she risk trusting Easton when she's been burned in the past?

#2870 A KISS AT THE MISTLETOE RODEO

Montana Mavericks: The Real Cowboys of Bronco Heights
by Kathy Douglass

During a rare hometown visit to Bronco for a holiday competition, rodeo superstar Geoff Burris is sidelined by an injury—and meets Stephanie Brandt. Geoff is captivated by the no-nonsense introvert. He'd never planned to put down roots, but when Stephanie is in his arms, all he can think about is forever...

#2871 TWELVE DATES OF CHRISTMAS

Sutter Creek, Montana • by Laurel Greer

When a local wilderness lodge almost cancels its Twelve Days of Christmas festival, Emma Halloran leaps at the chance to convince the owners of her vision for the business. But Luke Emerson has his own plans. As they work together, Luke and Emma are increasingly drawn to each other. Can these utter opposites unite over their shared passion this Christmas?

#2872 HIS BABY NO MATTER WHAT

Dawson Family Ranch • by Melissa Senate

Nothing will change how much Colt Dawson loves his baby boy. Not even the shocking news his deceased wife lied about Ryder's paternity. But confronting Ava Guthrie about his ex's sperm-donor scheme doesn't go as planned. Will Ava heal Colt's betrayed heart in time for a Wyoming family Christmas?

#2873 THE BEST MAN IN TEXAS

Forever, Texas • by Marie Ferrarella

Jason Eastwood and Adelyn Montenegro may have hit it off at a wedding, but neither of them is looking for love, not when they have careers and lives to establish. Still, as they work together to build the hospital that's meaningful to them both, the pull between them becomes hard to resist. Will they be able to put their preconceived ideas about relationships aside, or will she let the best man slip away?

#2874 THE COWBOY'S CHRISTMAS RETREAT

Top Dog Dude Ranch • by Catherine Mann

Riley Stewart has been jilted. He needs an understanding shoulder, so Riley invites his best friend, Lucy Snyder, and her son on his "honeymoon." But moonlit walks, romantic fires, the glow of Christmas lights—everything is conspiring against their "just friends" resolve. Will this fake honeymoon ignite the real spark Riley and Lucy have denied for so long?

SPECIAL EXCERPT FROM

HARLEQUIN

SPECIAL EDITION

Nothing will change how much Colt Dawson loves his baby boy. Not even the shocking news his deceased wife lied about Ryder's paternity. But confronting Ava Guthrie about his ex's sperm-donor scheme doesn't go as planned. Will Ava heal Colt's betrayed heart in time for a Wyoming family Christmas?

Read on for a sneak peek at
His Baby No Matter What,
the next book in the Dawson Family Ranch miniseries
by Melissa Senate!

"I wasn't planning on getting one," Ava said. "I figured it would be make me feel sad, celebrating all alone out at the ranch. My parents gone too young. And this year, my great-aunt gone before I even knew her. My best friend after the worst argument I've ever had. I love Christmas, but this is a weird one."

"Yeah, it is. And you're not alone. I'm here. Ryder's here. And like you said, you love Christmas. That house needs some serious cheering up. I want to get you a tree as a gift from me to you for our good deal."

"It *is* a good deal," she said. "Okay. A tree. I have a box of ornaments that I brought over in the move to the ranch."

He pulled out his phone, did some googling and found a Christmas-tree farm that also sold wreaths just ten minutes from here. He held up the site. "Let's go after Ryder's nap. While he's asleep, we can have that meeting—I mean, *talk*—about our arrangement. Set the agenda. The… What would you call it in noncorporate speak?"

She laughed. "Maybe it is a little nice having a CEO around here," she said, then took a bite of her sandwich. "You get things done, Colt Dawson."

He reached over and touched her hand and she squeezed it. Again he was struck by how close he felt to her. But he had to remember he was leaving in two and a half weeks, going back to Bear Ridge, back to his life. There was a 5 percent chance, probably less, that he'd ever leave Godfrey and Dawson. But he'd have this break, this Christmas with his son, on this alpaca ranch.

With a woman who made him think of reaching for the stars, even if he wouldn't.